CRONE TREKKING
IN COYOTE LAND

A Storymaking Book

Earth Blessings
to you —
Gwendolyn

Marilyn Burkhardt

Tree Goddess 2nd Century A.D., Mathura, Stone

CRONE TREKKING IN COYOTE LAND

A Storymaking Book

by

Gwendolyn Endicott

COVER ILLUSTRATION
"DEPTH READING"
Marilyn Burkhardt

DESIGN & PRODUCTION
Lorraine Ortiz

Attic
press

42130 Anderson Road
Nehalem, Oregon
97131

503/368-6389

For information, address Attic Press, at 42130 Anderson Road, Nehalem, Oregon 97131.
Library of Congress Catalog Card number: 2001118010
ISBN 0-9641187-3-4

Printed by Ecoprint, located in Portland, Oregon specializing in environmentally responsible printing.

Cover printed on 100% post-consumer recycled paper. Inside pages printed on 50% recycled paper, with a minimum of 10% post-consumer waste. Entire book printed with non-petroleum-based soy inks. The cover has not been laminated because of the toxic byproducts released into the environment from the lamination process.

Acknowledgment

In the beginning of all things, wisdom and knowledge were with the animals; for Tirawa, the One Above, did not speak directly to the people. Tirawa sent certain animals to tell the people that he showed himself through the beasts, and that from them, and from the stars and the sun and the moon, the people should learn. Tirawa spoke to the people through his works.

CHIEF LETAKOTS-LESA OF THE PAWNEE TRIBE

Special Thanks

to the people who through the millennia have passed on their stories
of the sacred Earth so that we do not forget,

to the children who receive from us the precious gift of our stories
and pass them on to the generations that follow,

to my family who encouraged in me both respect and love of the Earth,

to the artists who so willingly shared their talents
in illustrating the stories of this book:
Marilyn Burkhardt, Barbara Temple Ayres, Lane deMoll, Sam Harmon,
Barbara Matson, Clayton Rippey, Liza Jones, and Lola Sorensen,

to photographers Joe Balden, Gary Braasch, Carolyn Greenwood,
and Craig Spegel,

to graphic artist Lorraine Ortiz,

and to the three wise women who gave me response,
encouragement, and editorial correction:
Lane deMoll, Lola Sorensen, and Judy Bluehorse Skelton.

Contents

Story One 1

In Story One from the Chinook people, Coyote is going along the road of life when he meets Grandmother Cedar, who moves to her own rhythms in her own time. Coyote follows his impulse— and shows us the jam we get ourselves into when we think we control Nature and "lose sight" of our interdependence.

Mythical Musings:

Story Two 37

In Story Two from the Nehalem people, the Trickster Ice goes on a great hunt for the illusive white sea otter. He finds, instead, a mysterious woman who carries a woven basket at her center. White Sea Otter Woman helps us remember the sacredness of Source and our power as guardians.

Mythical Musings:

STORY THREE 73

In Story Three from the Haida people, a young prince and his friends set out on a fishing trip, full of youthful arrogance. The boys' disregard of custom and their thoughtless cruelty to a frog attracts the mournful wailing of Frog Woman, and soon the belly of the earth shakes in volcanic upheaval destroying the village—except for Old Woman and her daughter, who remember the sacredness of things and hear the voices of Nature Spirits. Frog Woman teaches regeneration.

Mythical Musings:

STORY FOUR 107

In Story Four from the Hopi people, Spider Woman looks out at the silent, empty earth. And in the deep purple light of the first dawn, she begins to sing. She spins a line from East to West. She spins a line from North to South. Then she sits in the center of these lines she has cast to the four horizons, and she sings in a voice that is exceptionally deep and sweet. She sings the songs of knowledge, wisdom, and love. Spider Woman shows us the way back home. She teaches us about connection, about beginnings and endings—and about weaving again.

Mythical Musings:

Introduction

Dancing down the beach, her feet barely touching the sand, my six month old pup catches sight of a congregation of crows on the sand ahead—the biggest crows I have ever seen. Ravens? I wonder. And what are they doing? There's no food in sight. It appears they are simply gathered to talk with each other—strutting their large black bodies, full of themselves, filling the space with sound and energy.

"Light'n!" I shout, trying to call the pup back, but she is already lost in the adventure of crashing a crow convention. For a moment I worry, as the crows squawk and complain, flying close over her vulnerable puppy head, telling her what they think of her intrusion in no uncertain terms. But then they fly on, close to the sand, talking to each other and the world in general as they go. I feel as if I almost understand what they are saying; then I fall back into being an outsider looking in on a crow world where things of importance are said with great conviction.

"Why do you insist on calling yourself a Crone?" my partner asked me some years ago. I could see him struggle uncomfortably with the image. In his mind's eye the face of his lover began to transform into a gnarly old woman. At fifty, it was a claiming I needed to do. It brought the freedom to let go of my attachment to outward appearance, and the approval that youthful beauty had attracted. For in the years to come this would not be my strength. Something else was growing very rapidly within me: a power that no longer depended on what others thought but was born instead from my own experience and passion.

The birth of Crone is not necessarily easy. For a woman who has been conditioned by centuries of patriarchy where she is valued for her youth and beauty—not her age or her wisdom or her power—it is often a painful birthing. My relationship did not survive the transformation. That was sixteen years ago. By now, I have no doubt that I will continue to grow into my Crone self until Kronia, Mother Time, calls me into the Otherworld. And although I feel more comfortable with her now than I did at fifty, I don't doubt that she will always be a challenge. For she calls me to my highest Truth— that is the measure. Not whether I am "right" or "wrong." What is a Crone? My friend, Melissa, says it succinctly: "I don't *represent* anybody. I am just me and I say what I see."

Some years ago, I came across an image on a greeting card by German artist, Rudi Hurzlmeier[1]—a crow/Crone walking across a barren landscape with a dazed, "over the edge" look on her face. "That's her," I thought, "That's how I feel when I walk through clear-cuts, that's how I feel when I hear foresters refer to them as "regen" (regeneration); that's how I feel in a world where the phrase "natural resources" has replaced wilderness. That's how I feel in a world where this appears to make sense to

Rudi Hurzlmeier

people. She became for me the persona of this book. She walks through Coyote Land, the place where I live. It is both an inner and an outer landscape—a tricky place, where we *do* make mistakes and where we have the opportunity to learn from them.

This book is a quartet of four major teaching stories about our relationship with Earth. Many other stories from cultures around the world, as well as my own stories, weave throughout the "Mythical Musings" that follow each story. I did not deliberately seek out Native American stories in choosing these four—nor did I, in the beginning, know how many stories there would be. Still, both the source and the number seem right.

Native American songs and stories were my first doorway into mythology. I was not interested in Greek mythology, the only mythology taught when I attended high school and college. In fact, I was repelled by the stories of violence, rape, and domination. Since most people thought Greek was synonymous with mythology, I had quite naturally assumed that I didn't like mythology. I was in my late thirties when I discovered the songs and stories of Native people. Their voices spoke to the part of me that was deeply in love with Earth. Not only did they see the magic and beauty that had nurtured me since a child, but there was something else harder to put into words—a Spirit reality, a *sacredness* that drew me deeper.

I started a Native American Literature class in the college where I taught, and brought in story tellers, poets, and writers. For twenty some years, Native American mythology became a part of almost every course I taught, even changing the shape of my "American" Literature classes. By the time I began teaching Introduction to Mythology, I had discovered that primal peoples all over the world had mythologies of relationship with the sacred Earth Mother. Students in my mythology classes went through an initial shock when they found not Greek but rather Australian Aboriginal, Native American, early Goddess cultures, ancient Sumerian, Hindu... I had fallen in love with mythology, a mythology that told the story of our relationship with the sacred Earth.

"But why bother with mythology at all?" people ask. Because symbolic language is a very powerful and ancient way of thinking that imprints deeply on the psyche, much like dream language. And because we have a wisdom heritage. The Earth is alive with the voices of those who have walked here before us. Many had deep relationships with the earth. Some were dreamers who understood sacredness and visualized harmony and beauty. Their teaching stories give us a heritage for "right relationship" with Earth. Not only do they speak to us of what we now call ecology—interrelatedness, sustainability, aliveness—but they teach us how to listen, how to hear the sacredness.

In finding our own stories and recreating the mythology of our relationship with Earth, we let go of centuries of conditioning that tells us we are separate and have control over all else. We reclaim our connection to the living whole. To be *indigenous* means "to be a part of." Although we cannot go back to an earlier time nor become people of another culture, still, it is not too late to become "indigenous" people. In fact, it may be the only way to heal ourselves and the Earth.

In many cultures, Four is an Earth number symbolizing Earth's living body: the four directions, the four sacred elements—earth, air, fire, and water. In the fourth teaching story of this book, *Spider Woman and the Making of Worlds,* Spider Woman sits at the center in the beginning of Time and casts a line to the Four—from East to West, from North to South—forming the foundation, the loom from which all else is woven. When that world goes wrong, she starts again: once more creating the foundation—the four connected to the center—once more teaching the stories of wisdom, love, and joy. The teaching stories of this book are a foundation for creating and re-creating your own stories, your personal mythology of relationship with Earth. This is the weaving you pass on to those who follow. This is re-generation.

Gwendolyn Endicott
February, 2001

Using this book as a loom
for the making of your own stories

Doorway Pages and Image Cards

Crone Trekking in Coyote Land may be read simply for the stories it contains or as a "workbook" to help you find your own stories. As a workbook, the approach is to go more deeply into each archetypal teaching story by following the images that attract you. I call these images "doorways" into the story. They will be different with each person just as the experience and stories of each person are different. The doorway pages that follow each of the major stories are meant to give both symbolic and literal space to the images that call to you. The language of mythology works through images and the play of those images on your imagination. When you dwell with an image, it begins to speak to your deep self, drawing up other images, stories, dreams, and sometimes emotions as well. This will often lead you into personal process and new integration. In this way, mythology is very similar to dreaming—both are the language of imagination, both are the language of soul.

If you choose to follow this approach as you go further into each story through the *Mythical Musings*, you will find other images that call to you—all reflections from the initial story. Making image cards allows you to play around with the images much as you would play with Tarot cards: shuffling them, seeing which one comes up for reflection, laying out a spread, rearranging them to form different patterns that help you tell your story in a new way and so on. If you are working with the stories in circle, combining these cards for group play brings in entirely new insights and possibilities. If there were a Fifth "chapter" to this book, it would contain your stories and images arranged in the patterns you wish to create. I imagine this Fifth chapter in the center, growing out of the Four. It is at the center that the Tree of Life grows. It is here, as well, that you grow, and from this place that your stories emerge.

Practicing

Most everyone accepts that stories and myths reflect cultural attitudes and beliefs. We often study them for this very reason: to understand another culture. Less often recognized is the power story and myth have in shaping and re-enforcing cultural and personal reality. Because they work at a level that touches emotion and imprints the deeper self, they become the "blueprints" for what we manifest. We choose whether to pass these imprints on—or re-create them. The exercises that follow each of the *Mythical Musings* offer suggestions for playing around with images and story, as well as attitudes and patterns of behavior. I have divided them into three different approaches, although they are not mutually exclusive and one often leads into another.

PRACTICE:
An exercise of "doing" to stimulate story, image, change of attitude or pattern of behavior

IN YOUR MUSE:
Suggestions for exploring images through your particular art form

MAKING RITE:
Ways of deepening the story through ritual

STORY ONE

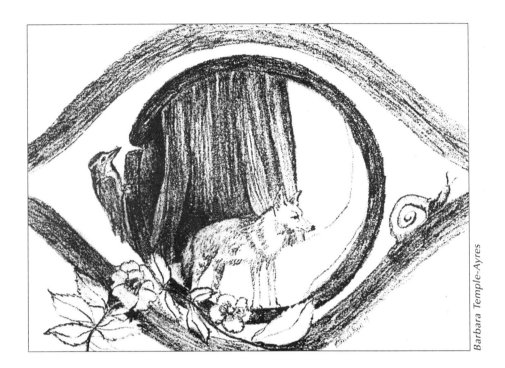

Barbara Temple-Ayres

COYOTE AND THE CEDAR TREE

It is essential that people realize at a rational and an intimate spiritual level that we come out of the Earth, that we don't exist separately from Her, that our health depends on Her health, so deeply are we linked.

CHARLENE SPRETNAK

Crone Trekking in Coyote Land

Sometimes I envy those of life's journeyers who trek the Himalayas, climbing in awesome beauty toward heaven—to come closer to their god. I browse their books, and look at their faces, radiant against infinite sky and snow. My own trekking happens much closer to home, in Nehalem country on the Oregon Coast, a place of water and wind and mud and storm; of ocean and forest and flooding rivers. And once in a while, a trip across the Coast Range to the big city of Portland for some special event. As trekking goes, I think it has its own style, but closer, perhaps, to the rhythms of coyote from the old tales who just journeys down the road of life and bumps into what happens.

I confess this Coyote influence in me has increased with age. As I have entered the Cronish years, calendars and schedules no longer rule time for me. I remember not in days and months and years, but more in episodes, in changes, in deaths and births of seasons, and of people, and in cycles of my own growing. This puts me in "mythic time" already, right along with coyote who inhabits not only the mythos of the region, but my neighborhood as well. At Wanderland, the forest where I live, the quiet of a summer night is often split suddenly by a high pitched, wild, coyote chorus, setting off the whole valley of dogs barking in frantic, unending, response. I remember once, in the middle of the night, jumping up in my sleeping bag the same instant my Malamute lunged in the door of the tent, both of us blown from sleep into each other's lap by the high pitched yelp of coyotes just 50 feet away. Another time I stood in my garden in broad daylight and listened to a coyote running through the forest no more than a few hundred feet away, going fast, yipping continuously as he went. I thought of the words that often begin a traditional coyote tale—"coyote was going there..."

There are six of us going along highway 53, packed comfortably into Tom's Dodge Caravan, winding our way back home. It is late. Only the highly motivated drive the curves of highway 53 at night, and if it is late enough, there are no log trucks. Then you can feel like you have the night all to yourself, taking it at your own speed. I am leaning against the window, watching the black shadows of clear cut hills slide by the stars. For the most part, we are silent, dwelling still with the evening's experience.

We have been to the city to hear Starhawk and Donna Reed speak of the film they are making about the life of archeologist, Marija Gimbutas, whose work gave back to us sacred images of the Goddess. "Remember, one person, one act does make a difference," Starhawk repeated again and again as she spoke of Gimbutus' work (and her own life as well). Only in hearing her words did I realize that I had almost forgotten—so powerful is the pull downward into hopelessness. My mind churned with the negative responses I had been getting to my own small project of documenting the gifts of the native second growth forest before we lose it: "It won't make any difference anyway;" "no one cares about plants, only the trees;" "you won't be able to do it;" "animals like clearcut." But worse yet, was the negative voice inside *me* that drained away my confidence and energy, beating me down with the same thoughts I battled against in others: "It won't make any difference." "You can't do it." "Why bother?"

And then, in the final moments of Starhawk's message—tired, ready to simply applaud and leave, 800 of us rose instead, pushed back our chairs and, at her suggestion, formed several concentric circles, "like a huge tree," "like the Tree of Life," she said. I thought of the giant cedar, branches as big as full grown trees, that still grows on my land and of the coastal rainforests that once grew dense with cedar. "What's the Tree of Life around here?" Starhawk asked. "Cedar," I said, as a chorus of voices around me responded "Douglas Fir." And then, by the sudden magic of suggestion, we felt our individual selves merge into the body of a giant Fir, deeply rooted in the earth, rising high above the auditorium where we stood, into the black of the night sky.

"Take what you hold most precious—your Dream," Starhawk directed us, "and put it in the center, in the heart of the tree." *The forest—let the forest live*, I pray.

Joining hands, we become a single moving body spiraling into the center, out of the center, into the center, out of the center. The drum beat becomes our heart beat. A chant rises and fills the auditorium: "She changes everything she touches; and everything She touches changes..." The spiral tightens as we dance, until it seems to burst from the center in a giant column of energy, and we stand, sweat pouring from our bodies, and watch—eyes closed—the blooming of the tree of life. *The sound of water; trees moving in the wind; birdsong; the long silent look of deer.*

Suddenly, Tom pulls the Caravan off the road and is out looking up at the night sky. "Meteor showers tonight," he comments. We stand for a moment on the mountain pass, a small group of six looking up into a night so clear it feels like our heads are in the dome of heaven. Occasionally, a star flash appears and disappears faster than we can call out.

Back in the car, we are immersed again in the silent rhythm of the drive, almost home, when suddenly our headlights outline what appears to be a shaggy pup running without a pause from the darkness on one side of the highway into the darkness on the other. "Coyote," Tom answers in unison with my question.

Yes, of course, Coyote, I think, skidding abruptly from the reality of highway 53 to a Coyote tale that had been weaving in and out of my awareness all evening.

STORY ONE

Coyote and the Cedar Tree

Over time, I have come to accept that I am a peculiar kind of storyteller. I don't collect stories and have a large number I carry around. Instead, stories come into my life and inhabit *me*. They grow inside me, sometimes over a long period of time, so that I begin to see and experience through them. The coyote story I had been dwelling with for several months comes from the oral tradition of the Chinook people of this North Coast region. In it Coyote has an interaction with the Tree of Life, in this case a Cedar, and gets himself in a jam.

Western Red Cedar, Wanderland

Carolyn Greenwood

The story begins with Coyote, just traveling along the road of life, trekking from Tillamook to Astoria, when he comes across those magical Nehalem lands and the forests of Neahkanie. This was in the days of the ancestors when forests were huge with giant trees, deep in their darkness and wild with animal sounds. As Coyote went deeper and deeper into the forest, his attention was caught by one tree in particular, a Cedar that stood as a giant even among giants. As Coyote came closer, he noticed that the body of this great tree was split, forming a cave-like opening, and as the cedar moved with the wind and the rest of the forest, it opened and closed, opened and closed.

Now Coyote was curious. He liked adventure. He liked a rush of energy. And he rarely thought of consequences. "Open," he cried to the Cedar tree. The tree opened. "Close," said Coyote. The tree closed. Coyote was sure he controlled the Cedar tree. He called out once more, "Open, Cedar." And when the Cedar opened this time, he hopped inside, never doubting that he could now determine the tree's movements. It was cool in the heart of the Cedar. The wood all around him was soft, crumbly, and red. But it wasn't long before he had had enough. He was impatient, ready to move on. "Open Cedar," he called. But nothing happened. "OPEN" he cried louder than before, kicking the side with his foot. But still nothing. Coyote sat down and took a moment to look at his situation. He was ingenious; he had the ability, as humans do, to imagine new possibilities and the power to involve other creatures in his plans.

One by one he called the birds, great and small. Each one tried, but failed, to make even a pin prick of a hole. In their effort, however, the bill of each bird was changed; some became shorter, some sharper, some curved, some blunted. As each bird was given its distinctive appearance, Coyote shouted out its name and sent it away: Wren, Eagle, Bluejay, Hawk, Dove, Sparrow... Finally came the Woodpecker. His bill sounded like a giant hammer, echoing through the forest. Coyote could see a speck of light as the tip of woodpecker's bill finally popped through the last layer of wood into the darkness of the central cave. But the hole was only about the size of a marble. He could see out with one eye, but he could not crawl through.

Coyote sat down and thought again. He was definitely in a tight spot. There was no way for him to stay in the same form and still get out of this mess. Leaping up, he started disassembling himself—feet, legs, body, arms, hands. head, ears, eyes, tail. Pushing each part out through the hole, he could hear it hit the ground on the outside of the tree.

Then, he was OUT. He would have kicked up his heels, if he'd had them, but obviously he had some reassembly work to do before he could do much of anything. So he got busy, putting his legs and feet back on his body, his head, nose and ears, and, of course, his tail. He was just about there, a whole new Coyote— when panic suddenly hit. The eyes. Where were the eyes? He felt around with his hands. He nosed around. They were nowhere. In a flash, he knew what had happened, old Raven had flown by and seeing those glittering balls on the ground had snatched them for himself.

Coyote was in a fix, but he hated, more than anything, being laughed at. He *hated* appearing foolish. And, of course, about that time he could hear someone coming down the path toward him. Acting quickly, he grabbed two pink petals from a wild rose bush that grew nearby and put them in for eyes.

Just then, he heard the laughter of an old woman; he heard her shout out: "Oh Coyote, you are a sight! How foolish you look with rose petals for eyes!"

Coyote thought fast. "It only looks foolish to you because you do not know what I can see with these eyes. These are special eyes. With them I see visions. With them I see spirit rays." The old woman was struck by the idea. "I would like to see spirit rays," she replied. "I will trade you. Your eyes for mine."

In a flash, Coyote had the woman's eyes and was off down the trail, going along as before on his way to the next adventure. "Old woman" he called back, You will be called snail because you must feel your way along the path, close to the earth. You will go slowly, carrying your home on your back." [1]

Barbara Temple-Ayres

Doorways Into The Story

Stories are much like mirrors. They reflect back both personal and cultural images. Because of this, different people will see different things in a story. What they see is almost always what is relevant to them, what the story is teaching them. To insist on one meaning violates the magic of a story, the aliveness, which grows and unfolds within the psyche. If you let them, the stories that are particularly relevant to you will attract you; in a sense, the story you need will find *you*. This is also why different stories will inhabit your consciousness at different times in your life. And why sometimes you feel the need for a new story.

If you by-pass analysis and enter a story through the images that stay in your consciousness after hearing it, you are more likely to discover what it is telling *you*. I call these images "doorways" into the story. Enter them gently without pushing too hard or demanding too much, and you will often discover that they unfold in ways that surprise you and offer you totally new insights. The doorway pages of this book offer you the space to enter the story in your own way before being influenced by my mythical musings.

Take a moment now to dwell with the images that stay with you from the story "Coyote and the Cedar Tree." There is no need to look back at the story or puzzle about it. You already know.

Finding the images:

1. Jot down the main images you remember from the story. Circle the three or four that attract you the most. Consider these your "doorways" into the story.

2. First give each image its own space by sketching it, one to a "doorway." ("Sketching" can be done abstractly with color or symbol as well as representationally).

3. If one of the images attracts you more than the others, focus on that one. Dwell with the image. Remember that the more attention you give an image, the more likely it is to unfold, but don't try to "figure it out."

Looking at the other side of the doorway:

1. After you have spent time dwelling with the image, create the back side of the card by decorating it with symbols or a design that reflects the "teachings" this image has for you.

2. Write an initiation story about passing through one of the doorways . (An initiation story involves going into new territory and the lessons learned.)

Ways to go more deeply with an image:

If you wish to go more deeply with this story, put the images on heavy paper, the size of Tarot Cards and add to them as you continue through the chapter. By the end of the chapter, you will have created a Coyote Deck of images that reveal to you the personal teachings of this story.

Here are some suggestions for creating image cards and going more deeply with them. Change or delete them as you choose. And remember that anywhere in this process, your own particular art form may take over: painting, poetry, writing, sculpting, mask making, song writing...Follow it.

1. Put the image in a special place and meditate or dream with it.

2. As you look at the image, freewrite your feelings and associations.

3. Give the image a title.

4. See it as an illustration in a book and write the story that goes with it.

5. Look at it as a Tarot card and write a description of its meaning.

6. If you decide to work with all three images, try giving each a title—as a Tarot Card or a chapter in a book might be titled. For example, "Following Impulse," "Rose Colored Glasses," "Coyote Jam."

7. Arrange the cards in any way that pleases you and tell the story they inspire.

In Circle

1. If you are working with a circle, shuffle everyone's images together and use them like a deck of cards, passing them around for everyone to choose from until they are gone. Follow the same process of laying them out in sequence. You can also invent rules. A "discard" pile might be interesting, where you can get rid of one but must take another.

2. In a circle, play around with the images through improvisational drama. Each choose an image. Say you choose "Coyote Leap." Get into the energy—dress like it, move like it, sound like it. A group of eight or so doing this with different aspects at once is wildly energizing!

Afterwards, pass the talking stick or write in your journal: What did this experience feel like in your body?

Creating your Coyote Deck

Add additional image cards as you finish the readings and exercises of this chapter. Follow the reflective lead—what images stay in your mind?

Giving Shape to What is Born

We dance around the tree of life
spiraling energy to the core.
Our visions rise like the wind,
giving shape to what is born.

For days after our journey to hear Starhawk, this chant drifts in and out of my consciousness. I am filled with the heightened energy of the spiral dance, the drumbeat, the faces shining back at me, each filled with their dreaming, and the sense of something larger growing, growing in the center, as we dance and dance around the tree of life.

A friend gives me a pair of earrings for my 64th birthday. On one is engraved an image of Coyote howling at the stars; on the other, people dancing around the tree of life. I laugh out loud, delighted by the synchronicity. "Did you know this is what I have been thinking about?" I ask her. "No," she replies. She is an old friend. My mythic musings rarely take her by surprise. "The jeweler suggested maybe I shouldn't give you Coyote since he is a trickster, but I said you knew about Coyote." "I'm not sure I'll ever know about Coyote," I say, "and I've been going around and around the tree of life. What *does* it mean?"

The problem is the tree means so *many* things. It is an ancient holographic image. That is, it has meaning for us on many levels at once. In some early cultures, when land was cleared for a village, a central tree was left to signify the power and unity of that community of people. This special tree might be an Ash, an Oak, an Apple, a Date Palm, a Sycamore, a Cedar, whatever tree grew with force in that region. The tree of life was also imaged in mythologies around the world as the "axis mundi," center pole of the planet. In Nordic mythology the world tree was called the *Yggdrasil.* The three goddesses of fate lived under the tree and guarded the golden apples which contained experience, knowledge, and eternal youth. The Fates taught humans how to inhabit "time": the lessons of the past and the good use of the present. The future was closely veiled and carried with it caution and warning against evil.

The tree of life also appears in stories around the world as the center of the garden of Paradise. In its roots lives a serpent. In the Hebrew tradition this primal garden is called *Heden* (Eden) meaning the "garden of delight." In our own bodies, the tree is again at the center of the garden. It is the magical staff, the caduceus, the tree of physical and spiritual health, entwined by two serpents rising (an ancient image that the medical profession borrowed for their logo). When the serpent climbs the spinal tree,

Kundalini blosssoms in each chakra and out the crown in bliss—and we are in the garden of Eden.

The tree symbolizes both unity of force and diversity of change. It is the "evolutionary tree" and the "family tree." At the center, It holds the force of Life. May polers dance around the tree to rejoice and participate in the rising energies of Spring. In the dance, the tree becomes the fertile staff of all nature. Christmas carolers sing their carols around the tree of lights, and in their song the tree be-

Lane deMoll

Tree of Life

comes the light of hope. Sun Dancers dance their prayers, moving round and round the central pole. In the dance, the tree becomes the lightening rod of visions. The central pole, the center of the circle, is "the oldest place," according to Jose Arguelles, "yet self renewing—pouring forth energy, yet ever present. It is the seed essence, the pearl of becoming." [2] Carl Jung called it the "scintilla," or soul spark, the image of Deity unfolding in nature, in the world, and in us. [3]

In Aboriginal imagination the vortex of dreaming is imaged as concentric circles spiraling out from a continuously renewing center. Painted on the earth, this is the "soak," the place of emergence. From this place the ancestors came, leaving their footprints on the soft ground. This is the intersection between dream time and waking time, the birthing place. From the ancestral imprints grow the living beings. In the same way, from our visions and dreams grow the realities of this world. Dancing the spiral in ritual takes us to the intersection between dreaming and waking. In that moment, our prayers touch and shape the future.

Still, it's a tricky business. When Coyote makes that leap into the center of the Cedar tree, he has no doubt that *he* is in charge, that he can control the tree. And in his usual, unabashed manner, he proceeds to yell out his commands: "open!" "close!" "give me this!" "give me that!" One of the delights of the story is the unexpected discovery that the tree has its own will, has its own rhythms, and that they may or may not coincide with our convenience. Coyote stories are often teaching stories although coyote, himself, does not usually get the lesson, for unconsciousness is part of what he teaches about. The lesson is *ours* to get. It is our unconsciousness. Coyote acts out for us the mess we get ourselves into when appetite and impulse control choice and action. For we, like Coyote, are shapers and transformers. We change things. And with that comes consequences.

 ## PRACTICE:
Sending Prayer

Many have forgotten how to pray. In fact, the very word "prayer" has negative meanings for some—connotations of rote recitation or of asking selfishly for what we want—kind of like asking Santa Claus for what will make us happy. Some people have suggested that I not use the word for these reasons. I think prayer, like many words, needs reclaiming. Chapter 5 of *The Spinning Wheel* explores in some detail the power of prayer as a way of attracting possibilities and manifesting intent. For here, think of prayer as a way of focusing intent and sending energy. Here are a few suggestions for focusing prayer:

1. Make a list of "most precious things." Choose one. Find a special stone to represent it. Hold the stone, seeing it as the essence of that precious thing, send it energy, seeing its strength and beauty grow. Take time to do this over a period of several days, then create a ritual for giving the prayer to the universe. For instance, tossing it into a pond or stream and releasing the prayer with your voice or an instrument.

2. Practice "tree magic." Stand or sit with your back against a tree. Breathe until you feel the separation between you and the tree disappear, and your bodies merge. On the exhale, allow your energy to follow the roots of the tree deeply into the earth. On the inhale, draw the energy up from the earth into your "trunk." On the exhale, allow the energy to follow the tree up into branching. Follow your own rhythm and timing. When the impulse moves you, sing out, call out, sound out, your prayers.

This practice will help you let go of the ego-self and connect you to universal health and balance—you don't have to know specifically what that is. The tree can teach you how to become the *vehicle* of prayer. Connected deeply through the three worlds, past/present/future, you become like a flute, giving voice to desire that rises through you and surrendering to the flowering of the tree of life.

MAKING RITE:

First do the focusing work of number 1, in "Practice." This can either be done alone or in circle.

Create sacred space by calling the four directions and the center, the above and the below. Honor the center as the tree of life. Place the stones in the center. Join hands and ground as a circle using the breath to send the energy down through your legs into the earth as roots, going more and more deeply; then drawing the energy up through the roots, through the body, and branching out into the sky. Now feel the circle as the tree of life, rooted deeply, reaching into the heavens.

Dance, chant, drum; move around the circle, calling out your prayers as the energy rises. Close the circle dance by putting your hands (body) against the earth and letting the energy flow back into the earth. Offer thanks and healing prayers to the earth. After the ritual, give the stones back to the earth or to the waters with the prayer that they be healing in the tree of life.

PRACTICE:
Grounding

As you practice, you will soon be able to "ground" with the earth no matter where you are: riding a bus, on a moment's break in your office, or in a city apartment. The exercise can easily be modified according to where you are. Energy may be visualized going down from your tailbone if you are sitting, or going down from your feet if you are standing. Here, again, is the basic movement:

Find a comfortable, safe place to sit, where you will be uninterrupted. Your back should be straight, your legs uncrossed. You may wish the back support of a chair or a wall; outside, a tree or a rock.

Breathe in and out, simply to relax your body and release tension. Become aware of the weight of your body against the earth, or chair, or floor. To become more conscious of your root, try rocking back and forth or in a circle, feeling your bottom against the floor. As your body relaxes, feel the warmth growing at the base of your spine, a glowing egg of energy.

Now on the exhale, visualize the breath flowing down your body and out in a root that pushes downward; feel the desire of your root to push deeply into the earth. Your root may branch as you go more deeply still. Continue to breathe deeply and exhale down through your roots into the earth.

When your roots break through into "the center of the earth," you will experience a flood of warm energy. Allow yourself to be effortlessly in this place. You are floating in a lake of warm energy at the heart of the mother, being washed and filled, washed and filled. Stay in this place as long as you wish. When you are ready, use your in-breath to draw up vibrant energy. Feel the roots going down from your body, and the warm earth energy flowing back up, filling your body and pushing out in branches from your crown. Feel the leaves and blossoms opening into the sky, the sun, the stars.

When you are ready, slowly bring your self back to present by focusing on your breath.

Add images to your Coyote Deck.

Joe Balden

GREENMAN
GROTTO

Joe Balden

clockwise from upper left:

GREENMAN MASK FROM LOMBOC

PORT ORFORD CEDAR

QUAN YIN'S CAULDRON

Craig Spegel

A Will of Her Own

In the dream, the tree is large with two massive branches, one to the right and one to the left. I can see into the branches as if they were an Australian Aboriginal Xray painting. In each branch, curled in fetal position, seed-like. sleeps a Tree God. I reach in and take them, one at a time, massaging them between my hands to awaken them. It is time for them to awaken.

When I first read the Coyote story, I was sure I had already met the Cedar tree. There is one so much like her that grows at Wanderland—an ancestor, hollow in the center, with two huge arms as large, themselves, as mature trees. I am told by those who still remember that once this area around Coal Creek in the Coast Range was known for the grove of giant Cedar that grew here. Their enormous stumps are now mother to mature trees some seventy years later. Many young Cedar, offspring of the old, grow here. They are mostly Western Red Cedar although recently we discovered a grove of Port Orford Cedar growing in a special place I call Greenman Grotto. Port Orford, an incense cedar, was once plentiful in the region, and a favorite of the Tillamook Indians for making canoes. Logging trucks carry a fungus from place to place on their tires that attacks the roots of these trees, and they are now dying out. Why it took us ten years to find this grove is somewhat of a mystery to me, although I have discovered, over the years, the extent of my own blindness and also that the forest reveals itself in its own time. Once we identified the Port Orford, I thought, "well, of course, if they were anywhere on this land, they would be in Greenman Grotto." In this place, a small forest stream cascades down into a deep clay cauldron and then goes underground, passing through the roots of the largest Port Orford Cedar in the grove.

Once, on an Easter morning, I came to this place to give thanks to the green life force, the miracle of Spring. After a few moments of prayer, I found myself transfixed by a phenomenon I could not explain. I stood and watched green light, glowing and moving through the bushes near the stream. The whole area was suffused with a radiance so alive that I could only stay in its intensity for a few moments. Another time, a woman camping near the stream, had a dream of a circle of dancing deer, and "waking" saw a bright light glowing through the tent wall that shifted into the smiling—but wild— face of a horned god. The next morning, she gave me a perfect description of the god Pan even though she had never heard of him before. We are surprised when we discover nature is spiritually alive only to the extent that we have forgotten. That there is so little wildness left, however, aids us in this forgetting. In his book, *Voices of of the*

First Day, Robert Lawlor points out what should be obvious to us: "The animating spiritual force that sustains life is manifested in nature's wild plants and animals. Without wilderness, the spiritual forces depart and life is doomed."[4]

When I decided to use Cedar to shingle The Forest House, I placed an offering of Cedar shingles in the ancestor tree's hollow center. "I am taking from you," I said. "And I give thanks. I will nurture Cedar, and spread Cedar seedlings on the land." I found a local, family run, shingle mill as a source, one that prided itself in using salvaged Cedar stumps and logs. It took me a year and a half to shingle my house. I held the shingles, one by one, fragrant and red, each like a single feather layered into a beautiful coat. The body of The Forest House now matches the red bodies of the trees that surround it. Still, I struggle with questions—how to take, and how not to take too much. A neighbor chose aluminum siding instead of wood, and the clearing of a larger patch of forest so he could access enough sun for at least some solar energy. It is hard to imagine calling a place with aluminum siding "The Forest House," but I can't say that my solution is better than his.

Native cultures teach us that what is required is *relationship* with nature. It is understood in their teachings that "nature" is alive. With an underlying assumption such as this, one takes and gives thanks—and cannot be oblivious of the source. Judy Bluehorse Skelton, a Native American Educator and herbalist, stood before the ancestor Cedar last summer and spoke for her people in thanking the tree for its abundant gifts of life, its special wood, its bark softened into clothing, its aromatic healing incense and medicine. For the Native People who lived in this area, Cedar was the source of life nurturing gifts. And as a life tree, it was sacred.

When Nature still has its own will, what is native to the place grows; what is not, dies. This *wild*ness or *wild*erness can literally be felt. Where I live you don't have to walk very far to pass from a native second growth forest into a "tree farm" or a clearcut. In doing so, most people sense that there is something radically different—something that doesn't have to do with the number of trees per acre. This experience would, of course, be more dramatic walking from an old growth forest into a tree farm. But it is not possible to walk through an old growth forest where I live.

A few months ago, a young man came to the Lower Nehalem Watershed Council meeting. He had come to tell the council that a beautiful native forest was being clearcut at the headwaters of a stream in the hills behind his house. Surely if the council were aware of it, they could stop such a violation from happening. He was particularly concerned about a grove of large Spruce trees—couldn't they, at least, be spared? Representatives from the Timber Companies responded; Oregon Department of Forestry responded. Representatives from the local towns responded. They all agreed: This forest is the private property of the timber company that owns it. It is a tree farm. It must be clearcut so that it can be replanted for maximum production. The clearcut is

CRONE TREKKING IN COYOTE LAND

in accordance with the Oregon State Forest Practices Act.

"But where can I go around here to find wilderness?" the young man asked. "Go to the State Park," he was told. And then, a city official added, "Don't you know it is illegal to walk up there? You were trespassing."

Sometimes it seems like the wildness has diminished in the patch of forest where I live, like a fragrance grown gradually more faint so that it is difficult to tell when or how it changed. Certainly, the forest has become more familiar to me. And the logging has come closer, the houses, as well. Ironically, after years of work, my own house also closes me off from the wildness that surrounds me. Sometimes, in the summer (you can see I've grown soft), I still set up my tent in the forest, so I can listen to the creek and hear the morning bird songs—and be startled awake by an animal cry, wild and strange. Still, I worry that the "voices" of nature are fading.

Today, however, in the midst of a November storm, the forest moves above me in great waves of wind and roar, reminding me that it does have a will of its own, much like the cougar that went screaming through one day last spring and left my heart pounding. I stand for a moment in the midst of the storm, listening to the voice of the forest—unable to separate sound of wind and rain from the rushing roar of Coal Creek and the trees themselves, raining water from their boughs. I am small in the belly of this moving force; in fact, I am nothing in the face of its power. Running for cover, I look from the windows of The Forest House across the space of garden, as the trees bow and swirl and rise, bow and swirl and rise as one moving body—a forest dancing in the wind and storm. The first poetry written in Sanskrit, I remember being told, was the sound of running water and wind in the trees. Today I am filled with poetry.

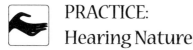 PRACTICE:
Hearing Nature

1. Spend a day listening to the "original poetry" of water (or wind). Use whatever medium is natural to you—words, painting, music—to create the elemental world you experienced.

2. Go to a special place in nature and surrender to that place. Do nothing. Simply "listen" with all your senses for at least an hour. Do this repeatedly over a period of a week. (You, of course, determine timing.) Notice feelings and attitudes. Physical sensations. Journal your experience.

3. The second week, go to the same spot. Open your heart and send your love to the place. Journal what you experience.

4. Often when we walk in Nature, we talk. Or if we are by ourselves, our mind is busy thinking and planning. Thich Nhat Hanh suggests the following breath meditation to help us stay present: Breathing in the sounds, smells, sight of the place; breath-

ing out, becoming the sounds, smells, sight... At the same time, filling the mind with the mantra: "I walk the living earth. I walk the living earth." (I usually find the mantra changing and soon I *am* the living earth.)

Add images to your Coyote Deck.

Through the Eyes of Snail Woman

Often, when I tell the story, Coyote and the Cedar Tree, people feel dissatisfied with the ending. "Wait a minute, that doesn't seem fair!" they say to me. "Coyote gets off free and just goes on down the trail, while the old woman, who just wants to see spirit, is turned into a snail!" "That's the way of a Coyote story," I reply. Coyote is not measured by standards of fairness and morality. Coyote is not funny. Nor is he kind. He is a Trickster, and often, you find you are the one who has been tricked.

This particular trick reminds me of a chapter in my own life. In my early fifties, I came into a period of very rapid spiritual growth, marked by an ecstatic experience of spirit flight that changed me forever. Afterwards, everything seemed to glow with exceptional beauty and archetypal importance. I felt changed, special, destined for some great role. I walked in a glow, much like looking through "rose colored glasses." In many ways, it was like the experience of first falling in love when you live in a bubble of self-absorption. I'm sure this must have been very irritating to many around me who had known me as an "ordinary" person. I did not know, at the time, that what I was going through was only the first step of my initiation. What followed was a long period of "tempering" in which I discovered that I was not the "Queen Bee" but simply a worker in the hive of the goddess. This tempering struck close to home and included loss of my lover, loss of friends, loss of a comfortable lifestyle, and many years of hard work, living close to the earth. By "close" I mean cold, mud, rain, rats, and discouragement close.

"But I thought following the path of spirit would be more glamorous than this!" I would sometimes wail in self-pity. Still, this was a time that took me deeply into myself. After thirty years of defining myself by my relationship to others, I was now challenged to relate to myself "one on one." My relationship with the earth also changed. Instead of going to nature for leisure and entertainment, I began to live with her—and to discover that what she did was not always for my convenience. During those years I became much like Snail Woman. She is not very glamorous. She travels close to the earth, moving slowly down the path, carrying her spiral home on her back, feeling her way as she goes.

Barbara Temple-Ayres

The ending of the Coyote story has to do with seeing in a new way. The only way coyote can get himself out of the jam he's in is to take himself apart, squeeze the parts through a narrow opening, and then reassemble himself. Even then, he can't go on until he finds new eyes—for just when he thought he had the situation figured out, Raven just happens to fly by. Now Raven is also a trickster. He can't resist bright shiny things, and so he is always stealing "the light." At this point, Coyote faces an unexpected turn of events. He finds that he, himself, has been tricked. In one swift moment, like a stroke of fate, he loses the ability to put himself back together in the same way. The imagery of the story reminds us that a crisis often *requires* not only that we transform but also that we acquire a new way of seeing .

Recently, I traveled across the Coast Range into the Willamette Valley, following Highway 22 toward Salem. Traveling new territory automatically gives you new eyes. I began to notice the soft green foliage of recently planted hillsides that intermingled with the clear cut. It was a pretty landscape, barren hills coming alive again in green. Then I began to sense that I was passing through what "nature" looks like now—where it is preserved. Not only did I realize how clearly nature is "managed"; as managed as the miles and miles of farmlands that extend through the valley, but I also saw that these hills, like the farmlands that grow corn or grass, grew one species—Hemlock. Since Douglas Fir has been so affected by Swiss Needle Cast in the Coast Range, more and more, Hemlock has replaced it as the most desirable species.

I am a fourth generation Oregonian. My grandchildren are the sixth generation of my family to live in Oregon. I grew up in native forests. Perhaps this is why it seems strikingly odd to me to have all the trees look alike. How many native species are absent in these hills, I began to wonder: certainly, many trees—Cedar, Spruce, Alder, Maple, Elderberry—and then the plants that cover the natural forest floor, so many, and yet not even noticed as they disappear in my lifetime. My Grandfather knew their names. It becomes increasingly difficult to find those who remember their names; their medicines have been even more deeply lost. Is this the best we can do? I wonder, as the road widens into a freeway and I pull off for a walking break at what I think is a rest stop.

Walking to the edge of a viewing area where I can see the valley below, I feel a peculiar vertigo sweep through me as if I were falling back in time. Hundreds of birds rise, soaring in orchestrated rhythms, and then settle again in the wetlands below. The air is filled with their calls and the sound of their wings. "Basket Slough National Wildlife Refuge" the sign reads, "2,492 acres of Wetlands Habitat." "Ah, a reservation for the wild," I think, not sure whether to be relieved or cynical. Still, it was beautiful— almost like standing in the 19th century, or maybe like looking through a zoo window at a magnificent wild beast in a recreated patch of its native habitat. Then I saw the sign, a large glass enclosed board. I stood reading it, again and again:

> *"The first rule of intelligent tinkering is not to lose any of the parts."*
>
> ALDO LEOPOLD
>
> **The earth is like a complex, finely tuned machine, made up of interrelated, dependent, plant and animal communities. When one of these plant or animal parts is lost to extinction, the community suffers and ultimately the diversity, stability, and overall health of this natural machine is weakened. Humans lose, too, for we rely on many of these "parts" for a variety of everyday needs—including food, medicine, clean air and water, and beauty.**

I copied it word for word and stashed it in my bag. Even though it was spoken in mechanistic language and was strictly from a human perspective, here on a sign in a "wild preserve" was a clear vision. Nature has *a whole body,* just as we do, all parts connected and important. When any one part is destroyed or sick, the whole suffers. If we made our decisions from that awareness, our whole way of treating the earth would change. But the last part—that the "beauty" of nature is an everyday human *need* necessary to health—I wanted to put that part in bold letters, hire a Goodyear Blimp, and fly it over the wildlife preserve, over the freeway, over the city of Salem, and on down the valley.

On my way home, I am driving through Tillamook when my lane of traffic stops abruptly. The rains today are hard—more, at times, than the windshield wipers can handle. I peer through the window, trying to see what is happening. We begin to move slowly forward when Luna, my Malamute friend, lunges from the back seat against me. She is sure something is seriously wrong. Then I get what it is. I am driving through water, a lot of it. In fact, my small Corolla feels like it is at sea, following in the wake of the four wheeler in front of me. "Just keep your foot on the gas and don't panic," I think, as Luna and I , face by face, try to see through the cascade of water. "I should have believed the reports that Tillamook was flooding," I think. Then we emerge on the other side of the lake, and I breathe again.

It's been a hard winter. Twenty inches more rain than normal since October. Whatever "normal" is. Water runs down the sides of the banks and hills. The rivers swell and flood pastures and roads. Road crews battle mud slides, thick as red molasses, filling dump truck after dump truck as the banks continue to slide into the roads. From a distance, the National News reports flooding in the Pacific Northwest where, they say, massive clearcuts have destroyed the earth's ability to absorb the water. They demonstrate this for viewers, showing how a forest—much like a sponge—can absorb,

Clearcut at the headwaters of Reflection Creek

whereas water runs faster and faster down a cleared surface, taking the earth with it. On the local news, there is no mention of cause. We move blindly, just trying to cope with the situation: "Flooding in Tillamook. Flooding in Nehalem. North Fork Road closed by a mudslide. Shiffman Road closed by slides. Detour by Highway 53."

Back home, I walk the lane that crosses through the forest—only to find that it has become a rushing creek. Debris and silt have plugged the culvert that should channel the tributary I call Reflection Creek under the road. New deposits of silt form mounds along the edges of the creek and along the lane. I walk a few hundred yards farther to watch it flow, a muddy torrent, into West Coal Creek. "More silt on the bottom of Reflection Creek," I worry. "Fish can't breathe or spawn in silt."

For three years I have participated in a local watershed council, commissioned by the Governor of Oregon, along with other similar councils across the state, to help restore salmon habitat—for the Coho salmon have disappeared from our streams. Last summer hundreds of acres in the hills above me were clear cut, including the headwaters of Reflection Creek, in accordance with the Oregon State Forest Practices Act.

Aboriginal cultures used story and myth to show people that unthinking acts against Nature would bring about catastrophe and their own personal suffering. Not that they, themselves, did not commit such acts. On the contrary, the prevalence of this theme in their stories indicates that human nature needs continual reminders. The myths of Western culture, however, have dismissed this attitude as "superstitious" and replaced it with myths of heroic domination. Coyote models the very delusion that so frequently afflicts us: a self-centered ego that believes we are separate from nature and that nature is here to serve us. We now walk the landscape of catastrophe. We have gotten ourselves into a "coyote jam." The story also tells us in shorthand what must be done in such a crisis. We must take ourselves apart and put ourselves back together again—with new eyes. The only way out is to change our vision.

But how do we do this? On the trickster path, we have already taken the first step—and that *is* getting ourselves into a jam. Robert Lawlor points out that "in witnessing the dying of the natural world around us and in ourselves, we have at last been able to see that the earth is living." In our time, Lawlor says, the word *indigenous*, which means "born from" or "being an integral part of a place," has come to symbolize the rediscovery that *our race is inseparable from earth and nature as a whole.* [5]

It seems like a long journey to come back around to what we once knew. Yet, this morning as I walk the forest in the early morning darkness, the single beam of my flashlight touching into small sparkling worlds of moss and fern, I move slowly, feeling much like snail woman. I cannot see far in any direction, but I breathe the fragrance of forest and earth, and my feet seem to sink more deeply into the softness. "I am a part of this living, breathing earth. I am indigenous to this place," I think over and over to myself. My heart opens and I feel myself relax into being at home.

 IN YOUR MUSE:

Coyote Land

The Trickster gives a twist, a turn, or an ending to events that we did not choose or expect. Almost always this creates change. There is often discomfort or pain and usually a lesson or a gift to be accepted. Select one of the following and freewrite (or follow your particular art form—painting, poetry, song...):

"Coyote Woman in Me"
"Rose Colored Glasses"
"Coyote Jam"
"The Bubble of Self-absorption"
"New Eyes"
A time you had to change form to get out of a jam
A time you were "tricked " by a life event
A time you were shaped by trying
A time you fell flat on your face
A moment when you looked foolish

What gifts did the Trickster experience give you?

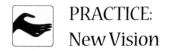

PRACTICE:
New Vision

1. Being Indigenous to Place

Seeing yourself as "part of" a place rather than just "living there" takes practice in changing the habits of mind that for centuries have reinforced separation. These are deeply imbedded in our ways of thinking, speaking, and acting. When we reshape them, we reshape our relationship with nature. This does not happen instantly. The "practice" sections of this book are ways to help accelerate that shift.

Map the area of the earth you call home. Instead of the usual focus on human creations (roads, towns, buildings) map only the natural terrain (hills, vegetation, rivers, ponds). Go as far back as you can imagine—to the earth as it was before human "development" of place. Sketch or name the wild-life that you know lived here.

Next, do a walking meditation in the area of your home. Keep your mind from thinking by repeating a mantra such as "I am the living earth" or "I am indigenous to this place." As you breathe, allowing the mantra to flow through you. Open your senses to the natural world: the wind, the sun, the vegetation, the birds, the temperature, the wild-life that lives here. Feel the energy of the place as it is (and was).

On your return, create a portrait of yourself as "indigenous." What touched you, became a part of you? What did you touch, become a part of? Try creating this as patterns of energy.

2. Place of Emergence

The place of birth, according to the Australian Aboriginal people, is your place of "emergence." The Aborigines journey back to that place to touch into their most powerful dreams and their art which is not separate from their dreaming.

(see p. 66, *The Spinning Wheel,* for further discussion.)

If you are able to return to your birth place, try doing the practice of Number 1 and include recording your dreams through art or journaling. Sleep outside on the earth, if this is possible.

———————

Add images to your Coyote Deck.

The Message of Grandmother Spruce

O n a hot August afternoon last summer, I made the short steep climb up an old logging road from the point overlooking Falcon Cove. Dripping sweat, I walked into a cool green forest world, so sheltered from summer sun that the earth still held the deep cool dampness of winter. Shivering from the sudden cool, I pulled on a jacket, and breathed deeply of the forest air.

I am a stranger here. Some of these trees have been here for hundreds of years, I think, looking around me—and more. A giant spruce grandmother stands before me, her branches large as mature trees, her trunk at least six feet in diameter. The small meadow where I stand is her front yard—a soft green mossy space, laced with tiny white stars of blooming miner's lettuce. "May I stay here for the night, with you, Grandmother—rocked by the sound of ocean and the great still voice of wind moving high in these trees?" The meadow is only a surface skin of green, I dis-cover as my tent stakes bend against rock at an inch or so into the earth. With sticks and rocks and ingenuity, I succeed in erecting my small purple dome at the foot of Grandmother Spruce.

Crown of Sitka Spruce Wanderland Rainforest

Joe Balden

I call myself into the presence of the circle. But each direction becomes a door-way, calling me deeper, as I begin to open to the place like a new lover, senses over-whelmed by its beauty, its surprises. Secret places, mossy bowers hidden by huge tree bodies. The smell of wildness. Large prints in the brown wet earth. Animals live here, knowing the soft moist places, the lush grassy spots, the dark safe thickets. This is a forest I breathe—a wildness where I am stranger, where I walk, but only partly see. How many are at home here—without me.

"The animals like clearcut," a Timber Industries' forester told me as we walked through Wanderland the day before. His company plans to clearcut hundreds of acres 1/4 mile from Wanderland in the soft, forested foothills of the Coal Creek watershed. "We thin a forest twice," he explained, "and then when it is 'mature' at 53 years, comes the 'final harvest.' " That's not even as old as me, I think, but cannot say it so he understands.

"How old are you?" I ask Spruce Grandmother. "Older than you," she echoes in my mind, "older than any around you, older even than your great grandparents would be;

older than the other trees who stand in this place, although some of their bodies are two, even three feet thick. Old enough to die and grow again. Old enough to be in my maturity."

My heart begins to open to the forest and the forest opens to me, leading me deeper, letting me see. "You have begun to take for granted," it tells me, "the beauty of the place where you live. Like an old lover, you think you know all its secrets. Now you've even begun to be annoyed by the little daily things—the neighbors' barking dogs, the VW bus that roars down the lane like a ground helicopter, the low flying helicopters that scan the forest; the rodents that battle for the house, the greenhouse, the car; the slugs and deer that eat the garden; the trees and 'brush' that overtake the trails and drives..."

Red markers on trees remind me of the network of property lines that go through this forest. Each human owner, drawn to it by its beauty, has the right to change it, even to destroy it. I have found my way back to the meadow again and stand listening to the ocean's voice, several hundred feet below. What a beautiful spot this would be for a house, my fantasy begins. Cut a few of those trees to let the sun in, and the salmon berry brush so you can see the ocean looking out from your deck...The meadow, the wildness, the forest secrets begin to recede as I add a hot tub, and start making trails.

Grandmother Spruce stands silent, her shadow dark as the late afternoon sun begins to filter through the canopy between me and the ocean's roar. What is it that she tells me in her silence? It's about my human arrogance again. It's the forest voice she speaks: "Yes, you have the power to change me, even to destroy

Sitka Spruce Wanderland Rainforest

Carolyn Greenwood

me, because you *own* me. But you know, in your body you know, the breath of a living forest, the smell of wildness. And for centuries before you, this knowing has lived. If you choose the relationship of *owning* me, you will lose me. But if you open your heart to me, I will open my secrets to you, letting you feel the wildness, the beating of my forest heart."

 ## PRACTICE:
Changing the language of relationship to earth

The Welsh people had a word for the feeling of love and belonging to the land— *hiraeth*. Families and clans that lived generation after generation in the same place experienced a deep knowing of the land that did not translate simply as "ownership." There is no parallel word to *hiraeth* in English.

Practice eliminating words of possession from your language when speaking of the earth. For instance, "my property," "my land," "Longview Fiber's forest," "my tree." This will make you aware of how deeply language reflects human control of the earth. Watch for the sneaky ones, like affirming someone else's "ownership." For instance, "This is a beautiful place you have here." Try changing the attitude through language: "You live in a beautiful place."

Add images to your Coyote Deck.

The Harpy Flock

"Haven't seen you lately," a friend commented, as I practically knocked her over, having blown in through the Deli door with the wind and rain. "I've been writing," I blurted out without thinking. "Writing what?" She was not going to let me get away easily. I peered at her from under the hood of my rain jacket. "A book," I said, feeling uncomfortable. "A book? What kind of book?" I'm holding my basket, inching down the aisle away from her, thinking, "Why didn't I just say I was out of town or sick or working or writing the newsletter for our women's circle?"

I feel stealthy. An inner voice nags at me: *Don't tell anyone about it yet. What if you fail? Why would people want to read what you have to say? and what right do you have to say it anyway? Are you an expert or something? A book? Geez there are so many books already. And look at how good they are. Who do you think you are?*

It should be easier this time. I've finished one book already. I remember, however, that it took months before I could call the "material" I was working on a book. "Say *book*," a friend insisted, correcting me every time I avoided the word. "Come on, say *book*." Gradually, *The Spinning Wheel* grew into a book. And now the negative voice adds, *"But what if the second one isn't as good as the first? What if you look foolish? What if you're laughed at like Coyote?"* For months I put it off, exploring, in the meantime, endless other possibilities: the garden, walks on the beach, Ben and Jerry's, talking to friends, trips to town, cleaning the house, reading, watching movies...

"If I write this and it doesn't work," I argued with myself, "I'm no worse off than if I didn't try." Finally, I sputtered forward into the first chapter—and got stuck. *"Why am I doing this?"* I asked myself, and picked up a book a friend had loaned me by Sandra Ingerman called *Soul Retrieval*. I often open books randomly rather than starting at the beginning. And then I am startled to find exactly what I need to hear. *"After a few months of writing* Soul Retrieval," I read, *"I found a negative voice in me chattering away: 'You don't know how to write. Nobody wants to hear what you have to say. Who do you think you are anyway?"*[6] Needless to say, I was riveted to the page. Someone suffered from the same disease I had. I felt like I was listening to my own voice.

Sometimes it seems to me there are whole legions of negative demons assigned solely to the task of holding down our creative energy. The larger the project, the more fierce their attack. Clarissa Pincola Estes calls them Harpies,[7] bird-headed "death goddesses." The name meant "snatchers," "pluckers." And that is exactly what they do: they peck away at us from the inside, snatching bits of confidence, plucking self esteem. If they were to come at us from the outside, we would be more likely to defend ourselves, to argue, to fight back. But from the inside, we mistakenly believe they are us. Years of criticism, comparison, and put-down now speak to us as our own voice.

Ingerman describes how she journeyed in discouragement to one of her spirit guides and said, "I can't write this book." The reply was: "That's fine. We'll find someone else to write it." She got the point. Her own beliefs and attitudes were sabotaging her creativity. "I had to either reach inside myself for tools to keep moving or else forfeit the work that was so close to my heart," she says. Ingerman clarified her intention: "I am going to write this book." She began to practice what she calls "mental calisthenics." Whenever the negative voice came up, she immediately made a positive statement to counter it. For example, if the voice said, "I don't have the ability to do this," she immediately "lifted" the heavy weight of that attitude with "I know I have the ability and I ask my mind and spirit to help me." She makes no claim that this is an easy process, but gradually she felt her creative voice gaining strength.

When you take on a creative project, especially a large one, you begin a journey into new territory. You also embark on a personal initiation that asks you to grow, to get bigger. One of the first tests in this initiation is believing the project will happen. Closely linked to that is self-confidence. The negative voices, the Harpies that peck at your self image, test you. They are part of the strengthening process. In the mythic movie, *Never Ending Story,* the boy makes a journey to rescue "Fantasia" (fantasy, imagination) from the disintegrating forces of "the nothing." One of his first initiations is to pass through the South Gate without losing confidence, even when the eye of truth sees through him. If even for a moment, he doubts himself, he fails the initiation. Once having passed through this gate, however, he must journey even more deeply through the Dismal Swamp of hopelessness, and not give up. The boy keeps going for the same reason Sandra Ingerman does. Because he cares so much. The choice is clear: "I had to either reach inside myself for the tools to keep moving or *forfeit the work that was so close to my heart.."* [8]

"What kept you going?" an interviewer asked me recently about Wanderland, a rainforest retreat and teaching place I have been creating for ten years. We had been talking about some of the tasks the project had required (none of which I had experience with): making a road, clearing a house site; putting in water and electric lines; building The Forest House from the ground up. And some of the tests that honed my endurance: living in tents, a 9x10 shed, even a greenhouse; the mud and rats; the day the tarps covering the newly framed house filled with water the size of a swimming pool, and pulled the walls down. The project had definitely offered me more than one "dismal swamp" experience.

"I couldn't go back," I answered her. "I loved the forest too much to let it go. And then there was the Beaver Mantra," I said, laughing at her puzzled look. It came from an incident that happened early on in the project. I was at the creek offering prayer, asking for guidance. I looked down at a beautiful beaver stick at the same moment that the words went through me: "Just take it gnaw by gnaw and don't get discouraged

by the big picture." Practicing this attitude helped me in the day by day work. There was no way to think about the whole project at once without being overwhelmed. But all I had to do was take it step by step. That was certainly enough to keep me busy. The Beaver Mantra also helped me have faith in the importance of one small rainforest project even though I didn't know how to change the bigger picture around me of clear cut hills and, the even bigger world environmental crisis. When we built the porch out from

BEAVER MANTRA: "Take it gnaw by gnaw and don't get discouraged by the big picture."

my room in The Forest House, we gathered beaver sticks from the creek, the bay, and the ocean, and made a beaver stick railing, both as a reminder and an honoring. The beaver has become totemic of this place, a dream built slowly, with work of the hands, gnaw by gnaw.

Yesterday, in the middle of writing this piece, I received a letter from a friend. In it was an absolutely beautiful story she had written about Wanderland, called "The Conversation in the Creek." I was delighted by it. Still, I found myself wandering aimlessly around the house feeling deflated. "What is the matter with me?" I wondered, as the voice inside me grew louder: *You can't write nearly that well. Why don't you just give it up?* The feeling of heaviness grew stronger as I cooked supper and delayed getting back to writing. About half way through the evening, I laughed out loud. "Wait a minute! What is this—a test? Of course, I can't write like that. That is my friend's voice. It is she who is speaking her truth with such clarity. It has nothing to do with *my voice* and my writing."

Comparing and measuring myself against others is a very strong imprint. It came from my culture, from the educational system, from my friends and family. I am, however, the place where it now lives. It is probably the most subtle and insidious of my personal Harpies. Sometimes its presence is marked only by a vague feeling of being inarticulate and clumsy; other times, by an uncomfortable heaviness in my body— "inferior!" it says. At its worst, it is the Harpy called "jealousy" that leaves me feeling utterly miserable.

"Practice," a Zen teacher once told me. "All we can do is continue to practice." It is a view that reminds you what being human is about. Patience and compassion are the best you can offer to yourself—especially when you think you should have "arrived" years ago.

PRACTICE:
Stopping Negativity

1. Not Passing On Negative Stories

Practice not passing on negative stories, stories of hopelessness, violence, and despair. Practice not repeating negative comments, comments that diminish other people, other people's hopes, other people's efforts. You will probably find this a difficult task because such negativity is all around us and inbedded in our habits of conversation, and in our ways of getting attention. At the end of each day, make a list of the negative stuff that got imbedded or stuck in your consciousness. Using a fire proof vessel, set the list on fire and see the negativity released by the flames into positive energy.

2. Recognizing The Negative Voice

The first step is to recognize the "negative voice" as literally "not-you." In fact, so much "not-you" that it eats away at you. Do this by exposing it, getting it outside of you. Try saying it aloud when you hear it and then countering it with an affirmative statement.

3. Acting Out The Harpy Flock

Over several days' time, jot down what the negative voice says. Then create an image and a name for each of the Harpy voices. (These images may become part of your Coyote Deck) For example, Voice: "I wish I had hair like that." Image: bird headed female with long blonde hair. Name: The Frustrated Princess. On the back of each card write or draw what affirms your own essence. Work with the process for awhile.

Now that you have the flock together, notice which ones recur frequently. Pull out those cards and put them in full view somewhere. Try journaling with them, for instance creating a dialogue with them or making one of them a central character in a story. Any of these processes will make them more obvious and get them on the outside. Oddly, it also gives them the attention they want and sometimes shuts them up.

 ## MAKING RITE:

In circle, create an improvisational play by acting out the Harpy Flock. Each person take one Harpy, preferably one you are trying to distance from yourself. The idea is to **exaggerate** its qualities, create a parody through speech and action. If you have a trunk of costumes, play around with dress as well. Remember you are all doing this at the same time, so there will be a cacophony of squawking Harpies. Keep exaggerating the qualities until they begin to seem ridiculous and laughter overtakes you. At the end of the play, ground the energy back to earth. Breathe to center yourself and listen inwardly. Pass the talking stick to share the Harpy experience. Pass it once more and each begin a single affirmative statement with "I am... ."

(More exercises in working with the shadow self can be found in The Spinning Wheel, *pp. 10, and 91-93.)*

 ## PRACTICE:
Creative Intention

Write out your creative intention in positive language. If possible keep it to a title or a single sentence. Post it where you will see it. Clarifying intention will strengthen your confidence and also help you manifest the project. This does not necessarily mean you have to tell others. A creative project has a dreaming and an incubation time. Speaking of it too early can dissipate the energy and subject it to outside scrutiny before it is ready.

I usually get titles before I get content. Both times I have felt a book wanting to be born, I have done a mock-up of the cover, complete with title, image, and my name. I put it in a box large enough to hold the pages as the book grows. In this way, it becomes more solidly manifest both in the writing and in my attitude toward it.

Add images to your Coyote Deck.

Vision Test

The distance between the forest
and Kaiser Permanente
measures farther than hours and miles
measures from trees breathing the sound of rain
to hallways winding in a spiral
oddly opalescent, like a nautilus shell
but labeled Clinic A, B, C, and D.

I circle around,
walk up and down.
They've added a new wing.
The familiar suddenly changes
into something else
but looks the same.
I breathe, quiet the panic,
pass an espresso stand,
try to look like I know where I am.
Then Clinic D suddenly appears
and I'm routinely charted in for an eye exam.

"This? or this?"
the doctor says,
"That? or that?"
clicking the letter landscapes
in and out of focus.
X's and Z's double and blur,
R's squash down into O's—
Then the whole line runs together
and I want to say they are trees
moving in the winter sky—
but don't.

"Cataract," the doctor says,
"in the left eye,
but don't worry about it,"
he adds quickly.
It's normal,"
and, in the pause,
I hear the words unspoken,
"for someone your age."

*I look longer than usual
in the mirror that night
into the eyes that are changing
into the face that is changing
into she who is still me.
And I worry.*

*"The inner eye grows clearer,"
I remember reading recently
in Clarissa Pinkola Estes,
as the outer eye, in aging, dims."
But the words tonight are hollow
as I stare at myself in the bright bathroom light.
And worry.*

*Toward morning a dream comes.
I am in the forest.
To the left, propped against the trees
is a painting canvas, larger than me.
I am covering it with color
but all I have are crayons
and I am frustrated that they won't blend,
that I have no skill.
The colors jar against each other rudely.
I give up and begin making spirals.
I am enjoying the movement
across the canvas spiraling*

*"Anyone can make spirals,"
I hear myself say, disparagingly.
Suddenly there is an eye,
real beyond my hands ability to create,
looking back at me from the canvas--
clear, open, like a flower radiant.
For a moment, I look into the eye of the soul,
and then, I am born into morning,
feeling gifted and whole.*

gwendolyn

WILD CARDS

Playing with the COYOTE DECK

You have now completed the Coyote Deck. The images of this deck reflect your relationship with the earth and yourself, particularly in areas of impulse, will, choice, and vision. Shuffle the deck and pull four cards, a fifth if you choose. Arrange the cards in any way you desire—in a sequence, a circle, a collage...freewrite the story of the cards. Follow your particular art in going deeper.

In Circle

1. If you are working with a circle, shuffle everyone's images together and use them like a deck of cards, passing them around for everyone to choose from until they are gone. Follow the same process of laying them out in sequence and telling or sketching their story. You can also invent rules. A "discard" pile might be interesting where you can get rid of one but must take another. Play around.

2. In a circle, play around with the images through aspecting and improvisational drama. Each choose an image. Get into the energy—dress like it, move like it, sound like it. A group of eight or so doing this with different aspects at once is wildly energizing! Afterwards, pass the talking stick or write in your journal. What did the experience feel like in your body?

Story Two

Barbara Matson

Ice and White Sea Otter Woman

Whatever I dig up of you, O Earth
May you have quick replenishment
May my thrust never
reach right into your vital points, your heart!

ATHARA VEDA XII

A Musing

I am fond of a type of thinking I call "musing." At the same time, it is a habit that sometimes gets me into trouble, especially when I am wandering around in a public place, a grocery store, for instance. I round the corner of an aisle abruptly—talking or gesturing, and come face to face with a stranger's eyes that see me—a wild haired crone talking to herself. I gather myself quickly into present; of course I know exactly what I am doing, just looking for that particular kind of salad dressing. My secret view is that elders "talk to themselves" not only because they are the most interesting people around, but because they have had time to develop the art of musing—a type of right hemisphere thinking, which, even though they find highly amusing, they must keep to themselves. Sanity, after all, is judged by one's adeptness at being present in the immediate trivia.

According to the ancient Greeks, the Muses were the source of "in-spiration," which meant, literally, breathing in "I-deas;" that is, breathing the deity (deas) into oneself.[1] The Muses were creative emanations of the Triune goddess (the wheel of life: Mother, Maiden, Crone). The Greeks said there were nine Muses—three times three, symbollically giving a sense of continuousness. Each Muse was the source of a particular "grace" or gift of creative expression. One Muse gave Memory—the kind of memory elder people are particularly gifted with—remembering the stories and the songs of the people so that they can be passed on generation to generation. When this Muse comes into you, the story blossoms and you become its instrument of expression. Something more than you is present. Something more, even, than the detail of the story. Other Muses in-spire through poetry, music (muse-ic), dance, sculpting, the making of pots, playing the flute, knowing the language of the stars. A Shrine of the Muses was built in Alexandria, called, of course, a "museum." One can only imagine the sacred art that filled this shrine, for it was destroyed by Christians who saw pagan art as profane. Later, archeologists excavated the sites of these old cultures, and sacred artifacts were placed in another kind of museum to be viewed by the curious of other cultures.

Although some find the whole idea of a Muse archaic and few contemporary poets admit to "invoking" the Muses, still artists have no trouble recognizing the feeling of being inhabited by a Muse. You feel exhilerated, inspired, larger than yourself. Time disappears; you stay up all night painting, writing, creating. Your body hurts, but you don't notice. You are impatient with interruptions. Nothing else matters. When you are done, you feel clean, complete, yet like an empty vessel.

This, of course, is what you experience when the Muse comes in with a rush. Most of us would like to know how to get that rush to happen more often or at least how to hang on to it. But She is fleet—and unpredictable. And often a nagging doubt comes right along with the emptiness of completing a project: maybe inspiration will never come again. In one of my favorite books, *The Mother's Songs*, Meinrad Craighead describes the elusiveness of "wisdom" in a muse-like way: "When I reach through the hole at my center , the gift eludes my grasp. Whatever it may be , I can possess it only as that mystery which beckons from the greatest distance and draws my heart deeper into the quest. The journey waxes full and then wanes dark, again and again. I stare into my hole focusing on a single point, waiting for her to dart wildly through my landscape." [2]

The way of thinking I call musing works much like Craighead's description, through focus and surrender. Whereas analysis would go for trying to figure out meaning, to "reach for it" as Craighead says, musing simply "focuses on a single point" and waits. Sometimes that "point" is a question; sometimes, simply an image, or a desire. Focus is increased by actually writing, drawing, painting, or collaging. The idea is to plant it like a seed in the unconscious; give it the time and space to unfold; and then to be receptive. Reflective time—meditating, browsing, walking, dreaming—is usually the most fertile ground.

Today, I am restless with story, unable to write. I decide to drive the forty miles to Tillamook to browse around the library, museum, and book store. Browsing has become one of my favorite ways of looking for inspiration. I like the randomness of it and the way it seems to attract synchronicity. For weeks I have been haunted by a Nehalem Indian story about a hunting party in pursuit of a white- faced sea otter. I am hoping to get closer to the story, to enter it. I don't know exactly what I am looking for but I decide to start with the Pioneer Museum. "I should have realized from the name that I wouldn't find much Indian culture here," I think to myself, as I walk from room to room filled with artifacts from the lives of the early Tillamook county settlers.

I begin to have the sensation that I am falling backwards into my own lifetime. I am a child in my grandparents' world, walking through the cavernous expanse of their old farmhouse. The stiff faces of my ancestors hang in heavy, ornate frames. How certain I was as a child that I would never be that old and severe. In a dim corner stands the old pump-organ; in another, the butter churn. The sweet/sour smell of the milk room fills my memory. And there is the hand pump. It was the magic of the hand pump that I loved the most: in the early morning, splashing my face with the icy water brought up from somewhere deep in the earth.

Then I walk into the next room filled with hunting weapons—guns and traps. When I was small, my father trapped mink and muskrat for cash. We were country folk and poor. I remember the sickish smell of raccoon fat boiling down for soap. The men of my family were hunters too. My grandfathers, my father, my uncles, my brothers, and then, my husband. Sometimes I went along for the adventure and the beauty of the cold autumn days. I wished for the success of the hunters. I remember, too, when that relationship with animals ended for me—the evening when my husband called me proudly to come see the deer he had shot. I was halfway down the basement stair, a young wife in a pink nightie with only the desire to please, when the cry escaped my throat. I had looked at the deer and seen only her beauty. I knew my husband's frustration and anger, but could not erase the truth of that spontaneous cry.

I walk through a door into a room filled with animals. The taxidermist's skill has frozen them life-like. They have been artfully arranged in replicas of their natural environments. I find myself standing in front of a sea otter mounted by itself in a glass case in the center of the room. I read the sign:

> *Sea Otter are now internationally protected. In the 18th century fur trade, they were considered the fur of choice, and trapped to extinction in the mid-1700's. Re-introduction has not been successful on the Oregon Coast.*

For a long time I stand looking at a beautiful animal about the size of a seal with rich, thick fur and a plump round body. Its face has that soul-eyed look of the seal. This one is looking back over its shoulder, as if it were being pursued.

STORY TWO

The Trickster Ice
and White Sea Otter Woman

arly morning mist hangs softly around Neahkahnie as the Nehalem men carry their canoes down the beach. With them is the trickster hero, Ice. When the first light silvered the ocean, the men slid their canoes into the water, catching the ocean at its deepest inward breath. They were hunters. These were the days when the ocean was filled with sea otter. Their coats were velvety and thick, twice as dense as fur seal. Their fur kept the people warm through the long, dark winters on the North Oregon coast and was always in demand for trading.

Hunting had been good. But there was an excitement among the men that had nothing to do with survival. A sea otter with a pure white face swam in these waters. All the men had glimpsed her; none had been able to kill her. Always, she eluded them, gliding, luminous and just out of reach. Some had tried spears, some had tried arrows. Both disappeared, just before reaching their target. And the sea otter—she, too, seemed to simply vanish into the mists before their eyes.

And so once more, on this day, the men saw her swimming, so close as if she deliberately enticed them farther and farther out to sea. And then she was gone. In the glimmer of the horizon, the men saw the faint outline of a shore, and as they drew closer, the glow of houses lit from within.

"Let's go," they said. "Let's see who lives there." They entered a house. They could not tell if lamps lit the room or if it was the woman herself who glowed for she looked so like the sea otter, luminous and beautiful. All around her on the walls were arrows and spears. The men knew they were looking at their own weapons.

One of the men approached the woman. He was young and his voice was strong. "Come with me," he said, "Come home with me." And the woman came with the man willingly, carrying only a small, woven basket. She held the basket on her lap as the men made the long journey homeward, back toward Neahkahnie.

They were almost home. They could see the dark shadow of Neahkahnie in the distance. The men were hungry. They had not eaten in a long time. They had gone to the house hoping to be fed, but the woman had made no offer to feed them. Ice began to mumble and complain. "I am just going to see what she has in the basket," he said. But the others warned him: "Do not bother her; you do not know her."

Ice did not listen. He tore the basket from her hands and ripped the top open. Then with a scream, he fell back in amazement. His legs would not hold him. In the basket he saw living things—little men and women. In fright and revulsion, he threw the basket over the side of the boat in the same moment that the woman, herself, dove.

"Those are my lucky lifetimes," she called out to them. "With them, you grow, you get old, but then you can become young again. You just keep on that way. You never have to die. Had we made it to shore, the Nehalem people would live forever."

"Ice," her voice echoed back across the waves, "you will journey long before you find your way home again." The men paddled and paddled, but the harder they paddled, the farther they drifted from Neahkahnie.[3]

Neahkahnie — "Where the Spirits Walk"

Doorways Into The Story

Stories are much like mirrors. They reflect back both personal and cultural images. Because of this, different people will see different things in a story. What they see is almost always what is relevant to them, what the story is teaching them. To insist on one meaning violates the magic of a story, the aliveness, which grows and unfolds within the psyche. If you let them, the stories that are particularly relevant to you will attract you; in a sense, the story you need will find *you*. This is also why different stories will inhabit your consciousness at different times in your life. And why sometimes you feel the need for a new story.

If you by-pass analysis and enter a story through the images that stay in your consciousness after hearing it, you are more likely to discover what it is telling *you*. I call these images "doorways" into the story. Enter them gently without pushing too hard or demanding too much, and you will often discover that they unfold in ways that surprise you and offer you totally new insights. The doorway pages of this book offer you the space to enter the story in your own way before being influenced by my mythical musings.

Take a moment now to dwell with the images that stay with you from the story. There is no need to look back at the story or puzzle about it. You already know.

Finding the images:

1. Jot down the main images you remember from the story. Circle the three or four that attract you the most. Consider these your "doorways" into the story.

2. First give each image its own space by sketching it, one to a "doorway." ("Sketching" can be done abstractly with color or symbol as well as representationally.)

3. If one of the images attracts you more than the others, focus on that one. Dwell with the image. Remember that the more attention you give an image, the more likely it is to unfold, but don't try to "figure it out."

Looking at the other side of the doorway:

1. After you have spent time dwelling with the image, create the back side of the card by decorating it with symbols or a design that reflects the "teachings" this image has for you.

2. Write an initiation story about passing through one of the doorways . (An initiation story involves going into new territory and the lessons learned.)

Ways to go more deeply with an image:

If you wish to go more deeply with this story, put the images on heavy paper, the size of Tarot Cards and add to them as you continue through the chapter. By the end of the chapter, you will have created a White Sea Otter Woman deck of images that reveal to you the personal teachings of this story.

Here are some suggestions for creating image cards and going more deeply with them. Change or delete them as you choose. And remember that anywhere in this process, your own particular art form may take over: painting, poetry, writing, sculpting, mask making, songwriting. Follow it.

1. Put the image in a special place and meditate or dream with it.

2. As you look at the image, freewrite your feelings and associations.

3. Give the image a title.

4. See it as an illustration in a book and write the story that goes with it.

5. Look at it as a Tarot card and write a description of its meaning.

6. If you decide to work with all three images, try giving each a title—as a Tarot Card or a chapter in a book might be titled.

7. Arrange the cards in any way that pleases you and tell the story they inspire.

In Circle

1. If you are working with a circle, shuffle everyone's images together and use them like a deck of cards, passing them around for everyone to choose from until they are gone. Follow the same process of laying them out in sequence. You can also invent rules. A "discard" pile might be interesting, where you can get rid of one but must take another.

2. In a circle, play around with the images through improvisational drama. Each choose an image. Get into the energy—dress like it, move like it, sound like it. A group of eight or so doing this with different aspects at once is wildly energizing!

Creating your White Sea Otter Woman Deck

Add additional image cards as you finish readings and exercises of this chapter. Follow the reflective lead—what images stay in your mind?

Sea Otter Musings

I am enamored of you, Sea Woman. Like quick silver you ride the waves just out of reach. O Spirit Woman, your radiance becomes the air around you so that even spears and arrows vanish. Diving deeply, disappearing, deeper still you go. Always you glide just beyond my grasp, until there is nothing left for me but to surrender and ask. Then I cross the shoreline of the spirit world and you are there. All I have to do is open the door and your radiance fills the room, like the full moon. You show me my weapons. Do I understand? Force cannot take you, only asking can. You come willingly, Woman of the Sea, carrying life in your basket, carrying life in your womb.

I, too, have pursued her—this White Sea Otter Woman of the Nehalem tale. I catch glimpses of her and still she eludes me. She has many faces. She is Spirit Woman, bringing a gift across the threshold—from the spirit world to the people. Her numinous beauty reminds me of the mysterious White Buffalo Woman of the Oglala Sioux. In the vision, White Buffalo Woman came from a distance in radiance and beauty singing. "As she sang, there came from her mouth a white cloud that was good to smell." Carved on one side of the sacred pipe she carried was a bison calf "to mean the earth that bears and feeds us." As the people watched her leave, suddenly "it was a white bison galloping away and snorting, and soon it was gone."[4] For the Sioux people the buffalo was a primary source of life, giver of food, clothing, shelter. Bufallo sustained life, like the fertile earth. Sea Otter, for the Nehalem, sustained life, like the fertile sea.

She is Mother of the Sea, the Sea Goddess who carries the source of life. She is called "Sedna" among Arctic peoples. If Sedna's rules are broken by overharvesting or killing animals that are too young, the Inuit people of Alaska say Sedna will withdraw her nourishment. In order to heal the breach and restore balance, the Shaman journeys to Sedna's home in the depths of the sea, and there combs Sedna's beautiful black hair until order and balance are restored.[5]

She is similar to the Selkie, "seal people," with luminous eyes and shimmering skins, whose stories have been told for centuries by people who live close to the sea. Their moonlike beauty especially attracts those who hunger to be whole. In Clarissa Pinkola Estes beautiful retelling of an Inuit Selkie story, it is a lonely hunter who captures the Seal Woman, stealing her seal skin while she dances naked in the moonlight. If the skin of the Selkie is stolen, legends say, she can do nothing else but come with you. But once she regains her skin, she is irresistably drawn back to the sea. The hunter in the Inuit story knows only the bitterness of life, his yearning for love. He is starving for what will fill him. And so, like Ice in the Nehalem story, he just takes what he wants. Most Selkie stories show, however, that no matter how strong the desire, this is a union that cannot be forced, for the Selkie does find her skin again, usually through the unknowing help of her child, and returns to the depths of the sea. Mara Freeman points out that this archetypal story pattern shows how "Through his conquest and domination of the Earth and her creatures, man has lost his soul; he is split in two and, at the end of the story, is left high and dry (on the land,) irrevocably separated from his feminine half (in the water)." [6]

She is Nature Spirit. She comes willingly if we ask. As a child, I simply lived within this reality. I sang and talked to trees, flowers, birds, animals, insects and felt their response. There was once a time, say many native traditions, when the animals (the ancestors) were people. This was the time before the world was fixed in form as it is now and everything was possible. Animals and people spoke the same language and there were few barriers between them. For the child, the world has not yet been given "fixed form." It makes total sense to children, for instance, to have "talking animal" books and films. Then I, like my culture, went through a long period of forgetting, so that now I also speak of experiences of remembering, sometimes with surprise, what I once knew. I remember, as a woman about fifty, standing in front of a tree, sending it love, and the shock of surprise when the energy rushed back at me, almost knocking me over. I remember hearing the singing that rose around and above the sound of the rushing creek. The "daughters of the creek" live at its headwaters, say the Haida story tellers. You can hear them singing.

And she is sea otter—simply and profoundly that. We see her floating on her back, holding her cub on her chest while she grooms its thick golden fur. Mostly she swims on her back so she can use her agile feet (with retractable claws much like a cat's) for cracking and eating shellfish. She holds two shellfish, cracking them against each other to get at the meat. For the harder ones, she uses a rock as a tool for cracking. She is shy and intelligent and not very fast. She forms a family with other females and cubs. They live in the kelp beds or around the rocks close to shore. The males swim together and have little to do with family life. She is unusual among sea mammals in that she has no outer layer of fat to help insulate her in the cold, she grows fur that is twice as dense as fur seal. She was easy to find and valuable to hunt.

The Nehalem story is an accurate prediction of what was to come historically. Intense hunting—particularly by Russia in the 18th century—led to virtual extinction of the sea otter along the Pacific Coast by the end of the 19th century. "Those were my lucky lifetimes," Sea Otter Woman cries out to Ice. "With them you never have to die." Ironically, Sea Otter has been successfully reintroduced in some areas of Alaska and along the central California Coast—but she has not returned to the Northern Pacific Coast.

 ## IN YOUR MUSE:

In ritual, light candles for a Muse and make an offering of song, music, poetry or symbolic objects—whatever seems appropriate to celebrate the muse you are invoking. Ground. Ask to be in-habited by the muse, to be inspired. Let go of expectations. Allow yourself time for walking, browsing, meditating. Be open to what comes and remember the Muse has its own timing.

Calling Back The Animals

I came from Oregon country folk. We raised vegetables, fruit, and animals. We hunted the land and fished the waters. The men talked about "Hunting Season" with excitement and described it by year and place: "The Steens back in '60"; "The Wallowas in '68"—and, of course, the adventures of the particular hunt were told for years afterward. Stocking our freezer with deer and elk was part of preparation for the winter. We had venison recipes for everything from swiss steak to mince meat pie. Most of the men of my family hunted for food and for sport. The home of one of my uncles is filled with beautiful animals—wild cat, cougar, mink, lynx—preserved in "natural" positions by taxidermy. Although hunting was part of everyday life for me, I am not a hunter. In a native tribe, I would have been one of those who sang to the animals to come, and who sang for the safety of the hunter.

The men of my family were integrous about the hunting relationship they had with the animals. There were certain understood rules: not to take the young; not to take too much and waste; not to cause unnecessary suffering. Still, this was a very different relationship than the native cultures who hunted the land before them. What disappeared was deep identification with the animals. What disappeared was seeing the animals as "superior" because they had gifts that made them more at home on the earth, gifts which, in right relationship with them, might be given to the people. What disappeared was belief in the reality of animal spirits that could be pleased or offended.

In the hunting songs of the Papago Indians of Southern Arizona, we experience both through hunter and deer—like being inside and outside the deer at the same time.

Ancient Mexican deer design

(The Deer)
The wind is rushing toward us
Far off,
Turning somersaults as it comes.
At the edge of the world
It stands still.

The clouds are coming toward us
Near by,
Spreading out as they come.
On the top of the mountain
They sit still.

(The Hunter)
Over there, far off, he runs
With his white forefeet
Through the brush.

Over there, near by, he runs,
With his nostrils open,
Over the bare ground.

The white tail climbing,
Seems like a streak on the rocks.
The black tail, striding,
Seems like a crack in the rocks.

(The Deer)
Here I come forth.
On the earth I fell over:
The snapping bow made me dizzy.
Here I come forth.
On the mountain I slipped:
The humming arrow made me dizzy. [7]

In the Papago tradition, if anyone kills an animal he does not need for food, it is a sin which the animal will punish with illness. If he has made the animal suffer by an unskilled arrow shot, or shows disrespect for its bones by leaving them for the dogs to drag around, he will suffer. In order for healing to occur, songs must be sung describing the animal with its particular characteristics, and repeating its name. According to the Papago, it does not matter if the songs are in praise or ridicule of the animal. The point is to visualize the animal, to evoke him, to make him real. In this way the animal's power is reasserted, dis-ease is healed, and balance restored.[8] When the animal's power is restored, the human's dis-ease (also loss of power) is healed. The healing goes both ways for it is the relationship itself that is healed.

Hunting cultures go back through 25,000 years of human history, shaping our oldest relationship with the animals. The rites and customs surrounding the hunt reflect clearly a culture's attitude toward nature. In fact, myths about the balance between people and nature frequently arise from these traditional hunting cultures and their very personal life/death relationship with the animals. The deer, in many of these cultures, represents an "interface" between the human world and the wild, natural, and unseen forces of nature—much as the seal in the Selkie stories or White Sea Otter

Woman in the Nehalem tale. One of the most powerful legends of the deer comes from the Celtic. It tells of the magnificent, and mysterious, White Stag who brings a message from the wild to the chosen few who are able to "hear."

The White Stag was first seen, the legend goes, by a hunter so old that he was covered with long white hair. Many days he had journeyed deeper and deeper into the forest following the tracks of what seemed to be an uncommonly large deer. His family was hungry. He needed meat to feed them. Then one afternoon, unexpectedly, he came face to face with the White Stag. The two stared at each other for long moments, in an awe of respect, for neither had seen the likes of the other before. Yet "when the grizzled face of the man met that of the stag, the thought of harming it never occurred to him. At length, they turned, and each walked quietly away through the forest from the direction he had come." [9] The old man returned to his family without food, and told his three sons of the magnificent creature he had seen. He told them that if they should see the stag, however, they must not harm it. Then he slept "as if dead" for three days, and for many weeks afterwards could not speak at all.

The three sons traveled to different regions and told the story of the White Stag, but as more and more people populated the land and wilderness receded, the stag moved ever deeper into the mountains and forests. Only a very few, the mystics and bards, were left who could see and hear the stag. Finally, only the tales remained to speak his message: a message "of brotherhood...of respect for man and creature, of respect for the earth and forest and moor and lake and stream and sea, which feed all living things." [10]

We no longer live in a traditional hunting culture, nor do our attitudes reflect the deep respect of that interaction. Mass production of animals, mass slaughter, and styrofoam packaged meat in supermarkets do, however, state a cultural attitude—one that leaves no room for empathy with the animal, and certainly no possibility of acknowledging animal spirits. If we are meat eaters, we must compartmentalize the source of our food, separating this awareness from our feelings. Such separation creates an emotional and psychological armoring in our relationship with animals. For an in-depth analysis and insight into the causes of this armoring toward nature, see Riane Eisler's comments in her book, *Sacred Pleasure* (1999).

A soul loss happens when we are cut off from the animals. Not only do we lose touch with the wildness in ourselves, but we also lose the magic, the wisdom of the animals. When we have no relationship with our power animals, in fact, do not even acknowledge them as real, says Sandra Ingerman, they go away. And *we* are diminished.[11] The contemporary shaman is a hunter of the fragmented soul, who calls the spirit animals, not to kill, not to take meat, but to ask for help in finding the way back into balance—back home.

Shortly before his death at age 87, my father had a dream so vivid and beautiful that he, a man who did not speak dreams, told it to anyone who would listen, including his brother, who thought it conclusive evidence that my father had lost his senses. In the dream, my father was running through the forest as if he, himself, were wild. He was holding his rifle, but he was not hunting. Instead he moved with the swiftness and grace of a cougar. He felt the power of his body and the exhilaration of his spirit. Frail and within a few weeks of dying, my father had come home in himself.

PRACTICE:
Calling Back the Animals

You need not be a shaman or hunter to start calling back the animals. It is a fairly simple practice that uses very practical magic: What is focused upon grows stronger. What is acknowledged becomes real.

 Call back the animals through spontaneous "song" or communication that happens in the moment of meeting. I describe this experience in *The Spinning Wheel* as "prayer on the breath of the moment:"

> *Breathing and humming, I relaxed into the sunlight. A louder hum whirred by my head, and I saw a small bird perched on a hemlock twig barely a foot away. "Can't be a Hummingbird," I thought, looking at it looking at me. Then she came, hovering, just inches in front of my eyes, standing still in vibration. "Just breathe," I thought. My prayer rose with the breath, and for a moment, filled the current between us: "Grandmother, sew up this wound. Stitch thiis overcoat with your quick beak. Grandmother, let my heart fly free. Grandmother, be with me." Then she was gone in a whir, into the clearing that was becoming the front yard garden at Wanderland.[11]*

IN YOUR MUSE:

Call back the animals through words, poems, songs, photography, sculpting, painting—whatever your creative muse. Start with where you live, for you have a stronger voice there that comes from your relationship with the place. One way to begin is by journaling who you see on your walks and excursions. Who is there but not visible? Spend time dwelling with one animal. What would it be like to be in that body to move as it moves; eat as it eats; make sound as it does. If you were this creature, what would you need around you? Play around with writing from inside the animal. Sketch the spirit of the animal. Make a mask of the animal.

MAKING RITE:

In circle, act out the process above by creating a "Dance of the Animals," wearing masks, using movement and sound.

 MAKING RITE:

Create a "Council of All Beings" with your community. The prototype of this deep ecology ritual was created by John Seed and Joanna Macy. The book they co-authored *Thinking Like a Mountain* is an excellent guide to putting together a ritual relevent to your community. Macy's book *Despair and Personal Power in the Nuclear Age,* offers a wealth of workable exercises that open and deepen connection to the earth and all beings.

Add images to your White Sea Otter Woman Deck

Re-membering Sea Otter

Historical Notes:

Natural Historian, Vinson Brown, tells how the sea otter, under attack from heavy hunting, constantly changed not only their living places but also their tactics for survival. First they retreated to kelp beds where it was difficult to see them and then to wild, rocky reefs where they were difficult to hunt. In Alaska and on the Central California coast, a few found particularly unassailable rocky fortresses where they developed a coordinated system of signaling the approach of danger. Here they remained totally hidden from man for several decades. Slowly, after international treaties were made to protect the sea otter, they began to come out from their hiding places and again allowed themselves to be seen by people.[12]

From John Sauter and Bruce Johnsoon, *Tillamook Indians:*

Somehow, through a process known only to shamans, man could communicate with the spirits and attain a degree of power over them. These magic powers were usually kept in a bag, made from sea-otter skin, which could be opened only by the shaman. These powers were said to contain human forms.[13]

The Story of the Unwelcome House Mate

In the midst of my sea otter musings, an artist, an elder in his seventies, told me this story spontaneously one evening about a sea otter I have come to think of as "Brutus." Some years back, a hulking male sea otter took up residence in the crawl space under his home, located on the rocky shoreline of Orcas Island. The sea otter obviously saw the crawl space as a cozy cave located quite fortunately in the middle of his habitat. Not only was the otter a noisy downstairs occupant, but within a few days of his occupancy, the fishy after-smell of his eating habits began to reek up through the floorboards into the house. The contest was on between man and sea otter.

The artist, a very ingenious man, first tried blocking the entrances with rock and wire. The otter simply removed or smashed the encumbrances. He called an exterminator who tried a giant "Have-a Heart" trap. After the otter tore it apart, the exterminator quit the job. He tried rigging up electrical wires, to give the otter electric shocks. The otter ripped the wires out. He tried peppering the underside of the house with mothballs, but the otter didn't seem to mind the perfume that made the whole house stink for weeks. Still, the artist did not give up. He rigged the area with a row of light bulbs and an old radio tuned to loud static. This he hooked up to a timer which switched on every four hours during the night. The otter, however, seemed to think this was an improvement in his living quarters and accepted the noise with equanimity.

Then the artist went for heavier ammunition. He engaged the services of a big dog in the neighborhood named Jake. The dog had the scruffy look of the Airedale and the strength of the Shepherd. The artist figured his attitude would "equal that of an Oakland Raiders line backer." One day when the otter was under the house, Jake came lumbering down the driveway as he often did. "I took him by the collar," said the artist, "and escorted him through the crawl hole. Then I panned a flashlight beam across the area. When the light hit Brutus, he turned and his eyes gleamed in the light. Jake's hair stood on end from his shoulders to his tail and he stiffened. 'Sic 'em, Jake, Go get'm!' I yelled. Jake abruptly turned and bolted out the opening. I ran after him, commanding him to return, but as I came around the house, I saw Jake bounding up the drive and on down the road. He never returned."

Finally, after weeks of battle, the artist squirted his housemate with ammonia, which to the otter must have seemed the most obnoxiously polluted water he had ever encountered. The otter left. Now telling the story, the artist just shakes his head in wonder not only at the persistence but at the intelligence of the animal.

Resident Sea Otter

CRONE TREKKING IN COYOTE LAND

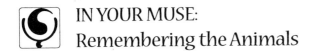

IN YOUR MUSE:
Remembering the Animals

Find out as much as you can about the animals and birds who have disappeared from where you live. Read their stories. Talk to the elders who knew these animals. Choose one animal to dwell with. In your muse, create a portrait of that animal.

Add images to your White Sea Otter Woman Deck

Room of Radiance

"In the Selkie legends," I told a friend, "there is a place in the depths of the sea, a 'room' filled with radiance, like going back to the source." "I know," he replied. "I've been there."

T he Nehalem tale of White Sea Otter is not the story of an ordinary hunt for sea otter skin any more than the hunt for the white stag in Celtic mythology is about venison, or the pursuit of the white whale is about whale blubber. This is an archetypal hunt for something much more illusive and extraordinary than the animal itself. The numinous whiteness tells us this—and the difficulty of the chase. Sea otter are slow and easy to hunt. This sea otter lures the men deeper and deeper, beyond the ordinary shorelines of reality. Then she vanishes into the mist. The houses glimmer, like a mirage on the horizon enticing them further still. They all enter one house. They know immediately that they have come to her home, that this is sea otter—and sea otter spirit. They are not surprised that she is woman; they are not surprised to have crossed the threshold into the spirit world.

Was it their desire that brought them to her—or did she, herself, call them to this place? She is silent. The scene, however, glows like an archetypal dream image: a luminous woman in the center of the room, hunting weapons hung, without power, on the wall. I like to imagine what it was like to open the door and cross the threshold into that room, to be with the hunters in that moment of meeting spirit. Seeing her, so beautiful, they forget even their hunger—for a moment. For a moment, they see that power is not weaponry and force, and simply stand helpless before her, present at the source. Then one, The Young Bold One, handsome in body and powerful in will, commands her: "You had better come along with me. Come home with me." Perhaps this is the voice of the trickster Ice, or perhaps it is simply the imprint of a culture where women obey male authority. The tale does not tell us. It tells only of the power of the man's youth and his maleness. Sea Otter woman goes willingly.

Every time I hear the story, I want to cry out to her: "No! Don't go! Don't Trust Them!" But there is an hypnotic quality about this part of the myth, an inevitability— almost like sleep walking. In the shifting light between night and day, in the pull of the tide away from the land, shapes change. We are in Dreamtime. It is not the body of a sea otter the men bring back, no rich, warm pelt to warm their children in cold—but rather a spirit woman, luminous and silent, who holds a precious basket. As woman, Sea Otter comes with the men as if they were her kin. Either she trusts them, or she moves in a trance. Perhaps this is "hunting magic," the power the shaman carried in the sea-otter skin bag. Or perhaps she already knows that her pelt has been "stolen"—

that she will be over-hunted for her skin, that she will be "taken."

Although she goes willingly in the story, the feeling is created both by her actions and by the imagery of "marriage" that she is moving from the wild to captivity. She carries in her basket the gift of her "many lifetimes": the seed, the life of her species. Do the men have a clue what responsibility they have undertaken as they row their canoes back home to their village at the foot of Neahkahnie Mountain? There is something about her that inspires their awe: "Do not bother her. You do not know her," they warn Ice. But in his hunger and impatience, he grabs what should not be taken.

Native American mythology reflects a reality where spirit and nature are not separate, and a time when beings of a "third type" lived. Neither human nor animal, they were both at once. There are frequent stories of animal spirits "marrying" humans and then bringing special gifts to them. In the story of Ice, the people lose this gift before it can be brought home to them. In many Selkie stories, however, a "marriage" does occur, and the gift takes the form of children, who meld the qualities of human and animal spirit—hence, are not separate from nature. The children in Selkie tales, being part seal spirit, sing the songs of the sea and know of its mysterious depths. Clarrisa Pinkola Estes' retelling of the Selkie story concludes with this beautiful description of the child and the child's relationship to Sea Goddess.

As time went on, he grew to be a mighty drummer and singer and a maker of stories, and it was said this all came to be because as a child he had survived being carried out to sea by the great seal spirits. Now, in the gray mists of morning, sometimes he can still be seen, with his kayak tethered, kneeling upon a certain rock in the sea, seeming to speak to a certain female seal who often comes near the shore. Though many have tried to hunt her, time after time, they have failed. She is known as Tanqigcaq, the bright one, the holy one, and it is said that though she be a seal, her eyes are capable of portraying those human looks, those wise and wild and loving looks... [14]

The child who comes of the marriage is the hope of the story. The child brings together animal and human, body and soul, masculine and feminine. The child blossoms with incredible creativity. The Muses are present in him. Spirit is present in him. Soul, however, lives in the depths of the sea. We get glimpses. We may visit through song, or prayer, or by letting our spirits journey there.

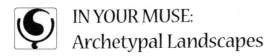

IN YOUR MUSE:
Archetypal Landscapes

1. In your particular art form create:

"The Doorway Between This World and the Spirit World"
"Threshold"
"Room of Radiance"

Add images to your White Sea Otter Woman Deck

In the Mother's House

The Angakok are the special ones. They can converse with the Sun and the Moon. They travel to the Underworld, going through rocks if need be. Indeed, the Angakok know the way to the floor of the ocean. That is why they are able to tell the story of Sedna, the Great Woman who lives at the Bottom of the Sea. They tell of Her before the change in Her calling name, when She was young and lived only on the land. And they tell of Her now, whose mercy and abundance we beg, soft and generous when we appease Her by combing Her flowing raven hair. CAROLYN MCIVER EDWARDS [15]

Sedna, known as the Sea Spirit Takankapsaluk among the Iglulik Eskimos, lives in a house at the bottom of the sea. Some say the house has no roof, that it is open at the top so that Sedna, from her place by the lamp, may watch the actions of the people. To her right, in the glow of the lamp, swim all the different kinds of sea animals the people hunt as game: whale, seal, sea otter, walrus. In this underwater pool of life, you can hear the puffing and blowing of the many creatures of the sea.

Sedna gives the people all good things: food, oil for light and fuel, warm furs for clothing and blankets. But if she is angered, she also sends the worst misfortunes— brutal storms, bad sicknesses, and sometimes she hides the animals deep in the sea, so the people go hungry. If Sedna is very angry, the shaman in journeying to her house, will find a heavy stone wall blocking his way. If he is able to kick down the wall, he will find Sedna sitting with her back to the lamp and to the animals in the pool. "Her hair hangs down loose all over one side of her face, a tangled, untidy mass hiding her eyes, so that she cannot see." The misdeeds and offenses of the people are dirt and impurities that cling to her body and hair. She is nearly suffocated by them. The shaman must take her by the shoulder and turn her to face the lamp and the animals swimming there. Then he must stroke her long black hair, which has become knotted and tangled. She has no hands to comb it, herself. When she is calm, her hair free and flowing, when she is in a kindlier mood, she takes the animals one by one and throws them on the floor. "Then it is as if a whirlpool arises in the passage, the water pours out from the pool and the animals, disappear in the sea." [16] Balance is restored and abundance returns once more.

And why is the sea spirit, Takanakapsaluk, so easily angered? Because she has memory of violation and pain. She was the beautiful land maiden, the Earth Goddess Avilayoq, the myth says, who dared to kayak with her "father" to the very edge of the sea, to ask for food for her people in the winter time. But as she stands, arms out-

Sedna

stretched, crying out her prayers to the tumult of sky and water, the Old Man shoves her into the sea. When she clings in terror to the side of the boat, Old Man cruelly cuts off her finger joints which fall, bleeding into the water. From the joints of Sedna's fingers, from her own dismembered body, grow the creatures of the sea, all of whom have flippers or fins— but none have fingers. This is how Sedna came to live in her house at the bottom of the sea, her raven black hair swirling in the currents; the sea creatures, who are her living body, hovering nearby in the glow of her lamp.

Who is this "Old Man" who would sacrifice his "daughter" to the sea? Perhaps he is the very hardship of life in this arctic environment, one that demands constant sacrifice for the simple gifts of food and warmth. Or perhaps the cruel detailing of the story is yet another mythic vestige of the Goddess wounded and exiled to the underworld by patriarchy (the "father" forces). Either way, the sacrificed Sedna, whose fluctuating moods determine the fortune of the people, becomes an extremely sensitive barometer of right relationship with the living earth. In the myth, She is Mother of the people. With all her heart, She desires their well being. She is also Mother of the creatures of earth and sea. "The misdeeds and offenses committed by men gather in dirt and impurity over her body."

When there is suffering and unbalance in the village above, the Iglulik shaman journeys down under to the House of Sedna to restore the balance and bring healing to the people. For the ordinary shaman, this journey is full of hardship and difficulty. For the very greatest, a way opens directly down: "He almost glides as if falling through a tube so fitted to his body that he can check his progress by pressing against the sides, and need not actually fall down with a rush. This tube is kept open for him by all the souls of his namesakes, until he returns on his way back to earth." [17]

Perhaps because of those who have journeyed before us and tell Sedna's story, if we ask with innocence of heart to heal our own unbalance, our own dis-ease, the way to the Mother opens. Most can journey quite easily to the place in the depths of themselves where the Goddess Sedna lives. I have journeyed there in dream and also with circles of women. We begin by telling her story. Then we create sacred space, ground, and breathe. We carry with us only a few suggestions: to feel what it is like to move as a seal through water; to dive deeply, knowing we know the way; and to offer our love to the Mother, by combing her long, black hair. The rest unfolds uniquely with each person. Some return full of radiance. Some receive a message. Some sit and weep simply from the power of meeting Her.

 ## MAKING RITE: Meeting The Mother

In circle, tell the story of Mother Sedna. Breathe, ground. See yourself standing by the ocean's shore, listening to the sound of the ocean waves. Feel the wind and spray on your face. You are watching the seals. So easily they move from the rocks to the water, playing, diving. You follow them, finding that you, too, move easily, gliding through the water. Deeper and deeper you swim, knowing the way. Soon you see the glow from Sedna's house and see the fishes hovering near in the luminous sea. Ask from your heart to enter. Offer Sedna your love by combing her long, black hair. Stay as long as you may and be open to receiving. When it is time, you will know the way back through the waters. Focus on your breath to come back to present.

Take time in circle to journal and/or paint.

Circle Closing: Break into partners. Take turns combing each other's hair (hair pics work well). Do this lovingly and with care. Feel yourself combing the hair of the goddess. It is important to take as long as you wish with this ritual.

(This is wonderful to incorporate with a Mother's Day ritual.)

 ## IN YOUR MUSE:

"Sedna's House"
"Sedna's Long Black Hair"
"Prayer to Mother Sedna"
"The Mother's Heart"

Add images to your White Sea Otter Woman Deck

The Mother's Hair

At night I stand in front of the oval mirror
despairing over my hair.
How has it grown so fine and thin?

Sinking through the edge of dream,
an enormous sexual energy fills me.
I am making love with the Green Man.
Then my mind thinks:
"This is really carnal!"
But I let the energy dance larger.

I am in a cave where my mother lies dying.
She is mourning the loss of her hair:
"It use to be thick and beautiful," she says.
Then we are dancing together,
hair swirling and swirling around us.

" Oh Mother, Mother Sedna,"
hear my prayer.
"Oh Mother, my mother,
let me comb your long black hair."
"Oh Mother, Seal Mother,
Let me fill your deep well."
Oh Mother, Ocean Mother,
Teach me to flow."

gwendolyn

Amy de Vargas

The Mother's Curse

The Mother's body is running
red molasses pours down the hills

The Mother's body is bleeding
rivers run red with silt

The Mother's body is dying
large gashes tear her skin
red dust shrouds the earth
around stumps of cedar
alder, hemlock, and spruce

O Ancient Fir, gone long before
do you hear the sound of her cry?
Do you hear her calling
sea-otter, silver salmon, sperm whale—

The basket has been ripped from her center
The Mother sounds out her curse
 in waves across the sea—

"It is forbidden to violate me."

gwendolyn

The Mother's Words of Power

When I was ten, I first heard of "the curse" from my Mother, who spoke of it to her sister on the phone in a tone that told me it was both shameful and unpleasant. I sensed it was some kind of secret word between women, but had only a vague notion what it meant. Somewhere around that time, my girl cousins from the city took me to the attic of their house to show me cast off, blood stained napkins and told me this terrible thing, the curse, would happen to me as well. I was shocked. I had no doubt that whatever it was that happened was unclean, painful—and bad. It had the same name as using bad words: "to curse." I was so appalled by the terrible unnaturalness of bleeding, something I associated only with wounding, that I prayed with all my heart that it would not happen to me. I was so successful at warding off the event that by the time I was 17, I began praying that it *would* happen to me. I prayed to the Father God for the blood experience of being a woman. He was probably the wrong one to ask.

I am continually surprised by what I find in Barbara Walker's *Woman's Encyclopedia of Myth and Secret.* Thinking about the curse White Sea Otter Woman calls out to Ice, I grabbed the book from the shelf. "It won't have anything on this kind of curse," I thought, and opened to "Curse, Mother's." "All death was brought about by the Goddess's word of destruction, as all birth was brought about by her word of creation. By virtue of motherhood, any woman could tap the verbal power of the Goddess." The Biblical Hannah rejoiced when she became a mother for now her "mouth was enlarged over her enemies." Maternity had given her curses irresistible power. Walker goes on with paragraph after paragraph of examples describing the power of the curse inflicted by the outrage of the goddess or of mothers. The power of such curses was made even more inevitable by the use of menstrual blood in the magic of implementing them.[17] The Mother's blood was the river of *both* life and death, just as the moon that pulls the tides of her monthly flow, continually died and was born again. Hers was the magic of renewal.

According to Scandinavian prophesy, the "Mutspell" (Mother Spell) would fall on violent patriarchal gods who ignored ancient customs and rules of morality, and who perpetuated cruel warfare. In Hindu mythology, the goddess, Durga, uses her "supersonic" hum to destroy the Asuras, demon armies, that symbolized aggressive masculine force. In the Christian Gnostic writings there is a similar belief in a" world destroying curse from a Great Mother disgusted with the cruel behavior of the gods she has created." In her outrage, she sends a great power from "the place where the firmament of woman is situated." [18]

What had filtered down to me from thousands of years of mythic history and cultural imprint was fear of woman's power—the repulsive unnaturalness of her menstrual blood, the evilness of her power voice (the curse, witchcraft, black magic...) and the heartless, Black Goddess of Death. "The Greek word for the effect of a mother's curse was *Miasma*, a kind of spiritual pollution, bringing slow but sure destruction."[19] What got lost in all of this was *why* the Goddess, the Mother, was outraged.

I would like to take that seventeen-year-old girl that I was, and slide her right through the generations of negativity my Grandmothers and Mother carried about the power of our blood. I would have her by-pass the thousands of years of fear and darkness Patriarchal cultures gave to woman—the helplessness and shame. She would look with surprise at the Death Goddess—blood smeared, evil old hag, separate from life—and know from her blood knowledge, from her earth knowing, that the cycle of life renews. She would look to the moon, this seventeen year old. Washed by its radiance, joined to generations of women who felt the life/death mystery of the goddess in themselves— I hear her calling: *Moon Mother, You, who pull the waters of the earth and of my body; who grow full with radiance and then let go—again and again shedding into darkness; You, who in becoming empty, grow fertile once more. Moon Mother, You who hold both life and death, teach me your wisdom.* This time, she would know, before age 50, the power of the feminine mystery—the full-bellied moon, the dark veiled night; the fertile Earth Mother whose body holds continual renewal. She would know that the curse was not the life force within her. She would know that "the curse" was the power of her own voice saying NO to the violation of what she holds sacred.

The Hopi tell of three worlds created by Grandmother Spider. Each time she spun out a new world, she wrapped around it her white cloak of wisdom and sang to the newly created, her songs of wisdom and her songs of love. Each time she gave the direction: Stay connected to source and sing back your love. Three times she destroyed what she had created because the people forgot. They became greedy, cruel, and violent. They forgot their connection to source. Four times, she created again. We are now in the fourth world, according to the Hopi, where once more we waver between forgetting and remembering.

For far more time than not, our attitude toward woman and toward the earth, symbolized by many cultures as the Earth Goddess, has been one of reverence. To show disrespect for her, to violate her, would bring bad luck. Myths from cultures that reverenced the earth even make clear what the most frequent violations are: 1) Taking too much or wasting. 2) Not acknowledging the ancestor spirits. 3) Killing the young, the source. 4) Carelessness—causing the suffering of other creatures. In the stories, we are warned, bidden ahead of time (fore bidden), not to commit these violations.

In Aboriginal mythologies, when the earth is violated, when the Mother is violated, the Mother's curse sounds through the land: sometimes the person suffers, sometimes the village is destroyed, sometimes the world is destroyed for life must begin again. Myths speak of this transformation happening elementally: through fire, through water, through earth-quake and destructive winds. All four elements—fire, water, earth, air—have the power of changing what is formed into something else. In the symbolism of our personal evolution, the same is true. Fire transforms us through creative energy (Kundalini); water changes us through the force of emotions; earth changes us when the structures (or our bodies) collapse; and air sweeps us clean of restrictive or destructive thought .

An Australian Aboriginal myth tells of a people who were taken back into the belly of creation because an "orphan" boy could not be satisfied. The boy developed an insatiable desire for a particular kind of lily root and was not satisfied by anything else. The people brought him other kind of roots and yams and even honey. They cooked these with care and love, but nothing made him happy. The people said to him "Why can't you stop crying? Will you always be crying then? Soon the Rainbow Serpent will hear you and eat us." Even though they told him this, he could not stop crying. He cried and cried. A Rainbow Serpent lived to the North. The Rainbow Serpent heard the boy's crying and thought, "Ah, that is the place where the orphan boy is always crying." She went underground to where the people lived. The people tried to spear the serpent. They tried to stop Her—but they could not. "That's it," they said. " Bad Luck. It's no good. The Rainbow Serpent will just have to eat us." The Rainbow Serpent swallowed all of the people, and then went underground with the people and the insatiable child within her belly. Under the earth, She sleeps. In the South, She sleeps— ready to reawaken.[20]

The men in the Nehalem tale are so close to home. Their canoes move as if entranced toward the shore. They see the great, dark shadow of Neahkahnie rising from the ocean. Then in a single moment all is changed by the insatiable appetite of the Trickster Ice who goes against the warnings of the other men and rips the basket containing life/death from Sea Otter's lap. It is clear in that moment that a violation has occurred, followed immediately by a Mother Curse. "*Ice, you will not find your way home,*" Sea Otter Woman calls out. The tide turns. The wind batters their bodies. The men rage at Ice for causing such misfortune, and the waves pull them farther and farther away from home. They, too, become "orphans."

In the epic cycle of Ice, this fateful interaction with Sea Otter triggers a long journey north. It is as if Ice and his men have fallen through the doorway of Time—only they are at the very beginning when beings are but crudely formed and must be taught about even their primary needs: how to find food, how to have sex, how to cook and eat. It is as if humanity is in its "childhood." Ice teaches the people about appetite and customs and relationship with nature. This is, of course, exactly what he, himself, needs to learn. I like to think that eventually he does find his way back home, but this is not the way Trickster tales usually work. Instead, at the end of the series of tales, he is simply melted by another Trickster, South Wind, completing the cycle, at least elementally, and leaving us to find our way home without him—maybe having learned the lesson that he teaches.

PRACTICE:
The Mother's Words of Power

1. Be aware of your conversations for a few days, watching for the subjects that "fire" your voice. When do you speak passionately, with force? From this, list what is important to you.

2. **Creating a Portrait of Yourself as Protectress**: The Mother is a Fierce Protectress of Life. Look back over the brainstorming you have done about what you hold precious (Chapter 1, under "Sending Prayer" as well as the exercise above).

Take some time in a quiet undisturbed place to breathe and ground. See those things you hold precious around you in your world. Continue to breathe and ground, feeling your tree of life strong, full of vitality. As you breathe, begin to visualize the energy flowing from you, nurturing what you hold precious. Feel yourself Protectress of this living world that you nurture.

Breathe, feeling strength flow through you. Call to the animals for help in protecting what is precious to you. Be open to what animal comes through you. How does it feel in your body. What powers does it give? Spend as long as you wish feeling the power of the Protectress within you. See yourself emanating the powers needed to protect the world you hold precious. Breathe yourself back and when you are ready sketch your portrait as Protectress. (Add this image to your White Sea Otter Woman Deck)

3. Imagine that you stand on a mountain top. Your voice is large enough to be heard by all. What do you say? Journal this.

MAKING RITE:
Words of Power

Circle members do the preliminary practice work of 1, 2 and 3. In circle, create a ritual that gives each person the space to express her words of power. If possible do this exercise outside. This forces you to call on the full power of your voice. The center of the circle may be used as the speaking place. One person at a time. If you wish, decorate this space symbolically with images of power and/or images of what is precious to you. Each person might also wish to adorn themselves in a way that evokes the power they feel within.

Circle breathes and grounds together. It is a valuable exercise to let the desire to speak lead people to the center rather than just taking turns. This can be facilitated by a simple lead in: "Now is the time when your words must be heard. Feel them rising within you. Step forward and say what it is you need to say." This is repeated as a lead in for each new person. Limit expression to a statement made forcefully (not a speech).

The role of the circle is to listen—not to comment. It does not matter if you agree or disagree. The circle may, however, ask to hear the words again, especially if there is hesitancy or self-consciousness. Simply say, "again," until you feel the power in the words. For closure, the circle may simply respond: "We hear you."

 IN YOUR MUSE:

1. In your particular art, create these Archetypal Portraits:

"Speaking the Mother's Words of Power"
"Goddess of Life/Death/Rebirth"

2. Recreate your menstrual myth.

Add images to your White Sea Otter Woman Deck

WILD CARDS

Playing with the WHITE SEA OTTER WOMAN DECK

You have now completed your White Sea Otter Woman Deck. The images of this deck reflect your relationship with the earth and yourself—particularly the balance between taking and giving, the sacredness of source, and the power of guardianship within you. Shuffle the deck and pull four cards, a fifth if you choose. Arrange the cards in any way you desire: in a sequence, a circle, a collage... Freewrite the story of the cards. Follow your Muse in going deeper.

In Circle

1. If you are working with a circle, shuffle everyone's images together and use them like a deck of cards, passing them around for everyone to choose from until they are gone. Follow the same process of laying them out in sequence and telling or sketching their story. You can also invent rules. A "discard" pile might be interesting, where you can get rid of one but must take another. Play around.

2. In a circle, play around with the images through improvisational drama. Each choose an image. For instance, "In the Mother's House," "the Mother's Words of Power," "The Hunt," or "Combing the Mother's Hair." Get into the energy—dress like it, move like it, sound like it. A group of eight or so doing this with different aspects at once is wildly energizing! Afterwards, pass the talking stick or write in your journal: What did this experience feel like in your body?

STORY THREE

Liza Jones

THE PRINCE AND FROG WOMAN

Remember, remember the sacredness of things

running streams and dwellings

the young within the nest

a hearth for sacred fire

the holy flame of fire

FROM THE HAKO, "INVOKING THE POWERS"[1]

Little Sam and the Frog Pond

At two and a half my grandson, Sam, has a major passion—balls and throwing balls. In fact, he has a ball collection that he keeps in a large card board box: golf balls, volley balls, basket balls, baseballs, hacky-sac balls, ping pong balls, and balls I have no names for. If you want to see his ball collection, he will throw them to you one at a time, each with the particular style he thinks goes with the ball, and with a certain amount of caution brought about from various catastrophes—a golf ball through the living room window, screams of protest from unsuspecting adults who had mistakenly assumed, as the baseball comes whirring through the air, that Sam has an ordinary two year-old pitch, and once, shattered glass from a ball that wasn't a ball at all, but a green glass float I had saved for years. Of course, anything that even remotely looks like a ball moves into throwing motion very fast when Sam is around.

One of Sam's favorite spots is the Frog Pond at the end of the Wanderland garden. An abundant frog population of various sizes and types co-habit this pond with rough skin newts, some that reach eight or nine inches long. But most interesting to Sam is that there's always a rock nearby with the zooming power of a ball. Sam is fast. No sooner did I point out a good-sized golden frog sitting on a stump looking at us, than Sam had a rock in motion. Luckily, the frog was faster than either Sam or me—plunking into the water at the same time as the rock. But I could see the glint in Sam's eyes. In a flash, he had become a two year old hunter. "No. Do not hit the frogs," I said. Still I could see the urge was almost irresistible. This time he reached for a stick. I tried another tactic. "It would make the frog hurt. Would you like me to hit *you* with a stick?" I said, picking one up as if to demonstrate. He got the point, but in a way I had not expected. Shock and disillusionment flashed across his face. In his eyes, I had changed from his loving grandmother to someone who would hurt him. I dropped the stick, and started over again, "Sam, It's not good to hurt other creatures..."

In this way, Sam and I trade lessons. I try to teach him sensitivity to other beings, and he is *my* most sensitive barometer of negativity. A humiliating but clear lesson in this happened a few months ago when my daughter and I were engrossed in one of those conversations that assume the children present aren't present—or if they are, they somehow can't hear or feel. Totally absorbed in showing her how irritating another person had been, I not only told her what was said, but the way it was said—full blasting the negative energy of the encounter at her, along with my own frustration and anger. I saw Sam look at me and then at her. His face crumpled and he began to cry loudly. He was heart-broken that his grandmother was attacking his mother with such negative force. How had she changed like this into some evil thing? It took us a long time to comfort him. I got the point. I had been passing on the experience with a negative force even larger than the original. It was the last time I told the story.

Sam continually reminds me of how sensitive children are. Understanding, however, that other beings are sensitive as well—that nature, itself, is sensitive—often must be taught . One of the most powerful ways to do this is by illustration. My daughter told me recently of walking into a large toy store with Sam and coming face to face with a whole wall of TV sets all playing the same violent cartoon. She wanted to grab Sam and run out of the store as fast as possible.

When she called me, she was still worrying: "I should have said something to the manager." We both agreed the answer to that was "yes." And that there was still time. Stories and images are powerful imprints that shape attitude and way of seeing. American cartoons often make pain abstract and unreal. They use violence as a way of entertaining. Why are we surprised, then, when children kill each other? Why are we shocked when they torture a dog or stone a cat for fun?

On New Year's Day, 2000, Sam developed a serious sinus/eye infection that threatened his eyesight and gave him a very high fever for days. He was hospitalized and fed antibiotics intravenously while his Mom and Dad took turns holding and rocking him night and day. Sick with concern, I spoke of Sam to a woman friend who is a healer. "Feed his eyes things he loves to see," she said. "Show him beauty." I was struck by the simplicity of what she said. This did not mean he didn't need the antibiotics. But what a lovely thing to do with him, and what a wonderful prescription: "Feed his eyes." Feed his eyes with the beauty of life—animals, birds, trees and plants; rivers and ocean and sky. Feed his eyes with the love of his parents and grandparents, and the community around him. Feed his eyes with images and stories and movies that nurture him by respecting life.

In a hauntingly beautiful legend from the Tlingit-Haida, a frog appears that reminds me of the golden frog Sam and I saw at the pond. Actually, three frogs appear: I think of the first one as green, an "everyday reality" frog; the second is HUGE and golden, with copper eyes, in fact, not a frog at all, but a handsome Frog Prince, wearing a layered hat; and the third—the third is the revered Frog Woman: "She wore a labret in her lower lip and held in her hand a cane topped with the picture of a frog." The story, however, begins with the people. This is a shortened telling of the tale as found in Mary Beck's *Heroes and Heroines in Tlingit-Haida Legend*.[2]

STORY THREE

The Prince and Frog Woman

O n a warm sunny day during Salmon season, a young prince and his three friends set out to spear some Salmon at a nearby creek. The prince was used to getting pretty much whatever he wanted and that day he had wheedled his parents into letting him take the Cormorant Hat. The Cormorant Hat was made from the skin of the Spotted Cormorant and carried with it special fishing magic. The hat had been passed down from generation to generation by the men of his family. His father warned him: "Be careful. A lot of responsibility goes along with wearing that hat." His grandmother warned him: "You are not mature enough to treat the hat with respect. Something bad might happen." But they did not stop him. They only called out to him once more as he hurried to meet his friends: "Be careful of the hat!"

The boys spent much of the day fishing and the hat, which was too big for the prince, was continually in the way—falling off into the water, getting in his eyes, tipping this way and that. Finally, he gave it a careless toss onto the bank. Toward evening, the boys began preparing a salmon for their dinner. But each time they placed a piece of it on the skunk cabbage leaf for baking, a green frog jumped right on the leaf. The prince, in disgust, kept tossing the frog in the bushes. The third time this happened, the exasperated prince threw the frog into the fire and as it hopped around in panic, he pinned it down with his sword.

"Why did you do that?" the youngest of the boys asked in dismay. "Now we're in for it!" He repeated what he had been taught about treating animals with respect. The prince, remembering the warnings of his father and grandmother about the Cormorant Hat, was for a moment subdued. "Oh don't listen to the tales of old women!" the oldest of the boys said. "They've been telling those stories for years." The boys watched the frog in fascination: "Look at him skittering around in there! Listen to him crackle!"

That night, the boys' sleep was disturbed by the eerie sound of a woman wailing, "Oh my child! Give me back my child. What have you done with my child." Several times in the night, they got up and searched the camp, but they could not find the woman anywhere. The next day as they paddled their way back home through the low hanging morning mists, the wailing followed them.

Sometimes, it seemed that it hovered right above their canoe. "Give me back my child! What have you done with my child."

When they were finally back to the village, the boys, who were by now really frightened, ran to the elders to tell them of the strange voice. The elders, however, were busy with more important things and dismissed their story as just the overly active imagination of teenage boys. Then, for days, the villagers, themselves, heard the wailing, now grown more desperate, "What have you done with my child? Give me back my child, or your village will be destroyed."

The people of the village were a little uneasy. A few even wondered if perhaps the boys had done some foolish thing. But only one woman listened. She began to go around and warn the others that something bad was going to happen, but they dismissed her as a foolish woman. The men laughed at her. The people continued about their everyday affairs.

Then the mountains began to rumble in the distance. Still the people did not believe. The roaring of the mountains grew louder. The woman took her daughter, who had just gone through her puberty rites, and went into a cave-like shelter she had built in the earth near her home. And there they stayed for many days as the earth shook and moved and the mountain poured rivers of fire across the land.

Finally, when a shroud of silence settled over them, the woman and daughter came out into a desolate world. Everything—everyone—had been destroyed. One day, when the woman returned to her dugout with water, she heard again the voice of the wailing woman: "I knew your uncles would avenge you, my son. The boys should have given your body back to me. But they destroyed it by fire, so your uncles have killed them by fire."

Several days later, the woman went about calling," Is anyone there? Has anyone survived the

Liza Jones

anger of the supernatural being?" After many days of searching, the old woman became desolate. She and her daughter packed up their things and set out looking for any living being. Finally, they found a village that was only half destroyed. There they found a canoe and some provisions and began their journey up stream, looking for a new place to camp.

The next morning they neared the place where the prince and his friends had fished. They saw a huge frog in the water. It looked like a human being and was wearing a layered hat. It's eyes shone like copper. As the frog swam away, they heard the wailing woman sing," Oh my child, Oh my child, your uncles are at peace now that they have destroyed the proud ones."

"They saw a huge frog in the water. It looked like a human being and was wearing a layered hat. Its eyes shone like copper."

Liza Jones

Then they saw her standing at a distance on the shore. "She wore a labret in her lower lip, and held in her hand a cane topped with a picture of a frog." The woman knew her at once: "This must be the revered Frog Woman," she said, "and the child that was killed was a frog." Then the woman understood that the volcano had been sent as punishment for disrespect of the frog. In this way, Frog Woman became Volcano Woman.

But the two women were very lonely and sad. "Why have we been saved? What good is life if we are all alone?" they asked. An eagle was called to them by their sorrow. They told him their story. "We, too, respect the frog. You will be at home with us," he told them. He took one under each wing and flew them to Eagle Village. The eagle then appeared to them as a handsome young man. He asked the mother for the honor of being the young woman's husband, for she was very beautiful and respected the sacred customs. Thus the two women became members of the Eagle Clan, where they held Frog or Volcano Woman in highest respect.

Doorways Into The Story

Stories are much like mirrors. They reflect back both personal and cultural images. Because of this, different people will see different things in a story. What they see is almost always what is relevant to them, what the story is teaching them. To insist on one meaning violates the magic of a story, the aliveness, which grows and unfolds within the psyche. If you let them, the stories that are particularly relevant to you will attract you; in a sense, the story you need will find *you*. This is also why different stories will inhabit your consciousness at different times in your life. And why sometimes you feel the need for a new story.

If you by-pass analysis and enter a story through the images that stay in your consciousness after hearing it, you are more likely to discover what it is telling *you*. I call these images "doorways" into the story. Enter them gently without pushing too hard or demanding too much, and you will often discover that they unfold in ways that surprise you and offer you totally new insights. The doorway pages of this book offer you the space to enter the story in your own way before being influenced by my mythical musings.

Take a moment now to dwell with the images that stay with you from the story. There is no need to look back at the story or puzzle about it. You already know.

Finding the images:

1. Jot down the main images you remember from the story. Circle the three or four that attract you the most. Consider these your "doorways" into the story.

2. First give each image its own space by sketching it, one to a "doorway." ("Sketching" can be done abstractly with color or symbol as well as representationally).

3. If one of the images attracts you more than the others, focus on that one. Dwell with the image. Remember that the more attention you give an image, the more likely it is to unfold, but don't try to "figure it out."

Looking at the other side of the doorway:

1. After you have spent time dwelling with the image, create the back side of the card by decorating it with symbols or a design that reflects the "teachings" this image has for you.

2. Add image cards to your deck that reflect the teachings of the story.

2. Write an initiation story about passing through one of the doorways . (An initiation story involves going into new territory and the lessons learned.)

Ways to go more deeply with an image:

1. Make a card for the image and put it in a special place. Meditate or dwell with the image. Dream with it.

2. As you look at the image, freewrite your feelings and associations.

3. Give the image a title.

4. See it as an illustration in a book and write the story that goes with it.

5. Look at it as a Tarot card and write a description of its meaning.

6. If you decide to work with all three images, try giving each a title—as a Tarot Card or a chapter in a book might be titled.

7. Arrange the cards in any way that pleases you and tell the story they inspire.

In Circle

1. If you are working with a circle, shuffle everyone's images together and use them like a deck of cards, passing them around for everyone to choose from until they are gone. Follow the same process of laying them out in sequence. You can also invent rules. A "discard" pile might be interesting, where you can get rid of one but must take another.

2. In a circle, play around with the images through improvisational drama. Each choose an image. Get into the energy—dress like it, move like it, sound like it. A group of eight or so doing this with different aspects at once is wildly energizing!

Creating your Frog Woman Deck

Add additional image cards as you finish readings and exercises of this chapter. Follow the reflective lead—what images stay in your mind?

Volcano (Frog) Woman

Old Mother Dragon swims through the waves,
Swallows red apples, sleeps in deep caves.
Twin winged Pythons, writhing in the rain,
Die, shedding their skins, then are born again!

WITCHES CHANT [3]

F rog and Volcano woman are, at first glance, such an unlikely combination. There is the initial jolt while we get over the size difference and our conditioning that large is more important, more powerful, than small. And then, there is such contrast between the cool, watery womb of froginess and the rumbling, molten fire-in-the-belly of volcano. Symbolism works through similarity, and the similarity here is that *both* contain the mysterious powers within the belly of the Great Mother.

Frog loves the watery womb of the earth: swamps, bogs, wet stream banks, ponds slimy with algae. Frog is colored like the earth in shades of green and brown, copper, gold, and red. From the belly of frog come streams of eggs, like strings of moonstones they float in the dark waters of the pond, waiting to be born. In a process that resembles the human embryo's development within the womb, frog births rapidly through evolutionary stages within the pond: egg, fish, amphibian. But what a strange amphibian she is—with a head that resembles a human, a big belly, and back legs that look like a newborn babe's with webbed toes.

Not surprising that from the beginnings of human mythology, Frog has been associated with the womb and nature's regenerative ability. Frog Woman images go back to Upper Paleolithic engravings and Neolithic carvings. Frog has a double resemblance: she looks like the fetus within the womb of the pond, and her body is all belly—with legs, of course. There are even references in mythology to frog as "wandering uterus." In Egyptian mythology, the Goddess Creatrix, Haquit was portrayed as a *woman with the head of a frog* and the frog was her hieroglyphic sign. For a moment, we see again through the eyes of Old Woman: "A woman stands on the shore of the stream. She holds a staff topped with the image of a frog. Her lower lip is made large by the piercing of a labret."

As Creatrix, the Egyptian Goddess Haquet is the giver of life and all that promotes fertility; and at the same time, she is the destructive powers of nature. The

Pre-Hispanic Mexican frog design from Michoacán.

two powers are not separate; together they turn the wheel of regeneration. In the Tlingit-Haida myth, the Creatrix is Volcano-Frog Woman, sometimes known as Dzelahrans. She is Earth Mother. Volcano Woman in the Tlingit-Haida is also the collective memory and the guardian of tribal tradition. [4]

The Egyptian mid-wife goddess, Heket (derived from Haquet), is also associated with the Frog. Her name comes from the word "heq," a tribal matriarch, a wise woman of pre-dynastic Egypt. In the tradition of mid-wifery, the old women, wise in healing and medicine, were responsible for birthing not only the body of the child into this world, but also the spirit. Heket, it was said, had command of the *hekau* or "Mother's Words of Power." She was protectress of the source. In Greek mythology, the Triune Goddess, Hecate, follows in this tradition. Often shown in her Crone aspect, Hecate's totem is frog. As wise old one, she births the new:

Praises be to the Frog!
Praises be to Old Heqt,
> *to our Hagia Sophia,*
> *Holy Mother of Wisdom!*

....

Our croaky Mother comes forth from primeval waters
> *green with life and potential,*
> *alert,*
Her throat pulsing
> *(swelling, ebbing*
> *swelling, ebbing)*
as She contemplates the All
from lotus pads and muddy banks.

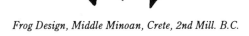

Frog Design, Middle Minoan, Crete, 2nd Mill. B.C.   DONNA WILSHIRE [5]

The frog magic in theTlingit-Haida legend unfolds on many of these layers at the same time. To begin with, there is something odd about the frog who insists on jumping into the middle of the boys' food preparation. We have already seen the prince treat the Cormorant Hat carelessly, tossing it aside with no respect. In addition, do we really know the boys were following custom in preparing and cooking the fish? The persistently annoying behavior of the frog is the first indication in the story that the balance has been disturbed. The story tells us that frog is respected in the customs of the people. This time the prince is not just careless, but cruel. This is an even greater disrespect not only of tribal customs but of the species of frog—and perhaps, the spirits of the waters as well. In India and Tibet, frogs belong to the mysterious realm of the "nagas," water spirits, with a kingdom and rulers of their own represented on earth by both snakes and frogs. The violation of frog brings upon the boys the mournful wailing of Frog Woman. When the people do not listen, for the elders, too, have lost their way, the "curse of the mother" falls upon the village.

Rumbling comes from the great belly of the mountain. The body of the Earth begins to shake. Streams of fire pour from her mouth. Red hot magma flows from her deepest core. Ancient earth dragon destroys and creates once more. Iridescent lava in rainbow black rolls down over the green of forest and village, turning life to ash and stone. Only the seed is left to start again. Hallie Austen describes the stark landscape created by Pele, Hawaiian Volcano Goddess—a world black like the night sky, inhabited only by Grandmother Spider: "For a while after the lava fields cool, large rick-rack spiders are their only inhabitants. They are the guardians of this sacred place, weaving the design of new life, laying the groundwork for what is to come. And then gradually tiny shoots sprout up on Pele's skin, growing to become ferns, grass, bushes, and then trees, until a whole new land is created."[6]

The Volcano Goddess is fire in the belly of the Mother; she is the heat of transformation that burns away the old and sparks the new. She is out-rage, rage expressed out—"dragon's breath," so to speak. She is Kali born from the brow of Durga in her outrage at the aggression of the Asuras—demon forces of dominance and control. She is you when you speak what is true from your gut and speak it with passion. She is the Phoenix—"fire-eagle." She is spirit rising again from the ashes.

In the Tlingit-Haida story, Old Woman and her daughter rise above the ashes of the village on the wings of Eagle, but only after considerable effort and grief of their own. The Death Goddess is not easy; She most often brings with her pain, suffering, grief, loss. The two women experience all of these. They cared about the people of their tribe. They do not want to be left all alone. They do not know what is going to happen to them. This is a severe initiation, and a stark underworld scene. The whole village and the landscape as well are dead. They cannot go back. In the story, Mother/daughter carry with them, not only the seed of life but the "seed-knowing" of their culture: they know what is sacred and they know correct relationship to the sacred.

> *Old Woman—*
> *She heard the earth crying*
> *Old Woman—*
> *She heard the voice of water spirits*
> *Old Woman—*
> *She said what she knew*
> *Then she went ahead*
> *And did what she needed to.*

CRONE TREKKING IN COYOTE LAND

Mother/daughter successfully pass through the maze of trials and tests and come back home again in an entirely new place. Volcano (Frog) Mother has mid-wifed their birth into the new. There is a particular beauty in the story's ending, an archetypal completion. Symbolically, the two women, in being adopted by the eagle, enter a new way of seeing that allows them to let go of a landscape of loss and grief and to focus on the renewal that is happening. The same archetypal language is used in the Nordic Runes where Initiation (Perth) is symbolized by the eagle and has the quality of "rising above," "seeing from a distance," "gaining broader vision." This rune is also associated with the Phoenix, the mystical bird that transforms by consuming itself in the fire and then rising from its own ashes (Volcano Woman).

The Frog Woman legend is an initiation tale—both of initiation completed by the Old Woman and daughter, and of initiation failed by the culture. For in the story, it is not just the prince who fails the test; it is the whole village, represented by elders who have no time to listen to the youth, and who have become careless about the rites of initiation that would pass down what the people hold sacred. The "prince" represents not only the next generation of those who should know and carry the responsibility, but also a culture that has gone off course, that has lost respect for the Mother. They arrogantly dismiss the grieving of Frog Mother; they scorn Old Woman's intuition and warning.

The Mother's Voice is heard in the wailing of Frog Woman, in the warnings of Old Woman, and finally, in the mountain's roar. When the volcano erupts in molten fire, we are reminded that nature has her own cycles, her own time—and that she *will* change the forms. Arrogance is struck dumb. In the story, the interaction between nature and the people is very immediate: violation brings a warning and then vengeance before balance is restored. "Has anyone survived the anger of the supernatural being?" Old Woman calls out as she searches the desolate landscape. But there is no one. Then she hears the wailing woman sing out to the frog, "Oh my child! Oh my child! Your uncles are at peace now that they have destroyed the proud ones."

Can we think our actions bring on so powerful a natural event? Can nature be angered? Primal cultures say "yes." Science and rationalism say "no." In fact, such an attitude is regarded as superstition. In cultures, however, that do not have such an immediate interaction with nature, there is much less fear of consequences and much more an illusion of control. Still, "bad luck" *does* regularly follow careless, arrogant action—as the story points out. The consequences are all around us in barren landscapes, flooding, mud slides, pollution of water and air, death of species—and in even larger ecological and nuclear catastrophes. In a recent article, Ed Ayres points out the generally unacknowledged link between global warming and "natural catastrophes": "During the last years of the twentieth century an unprecedented 2,144 tornadoes struck the United States, and 300 million people were driven from their homes by the Yangtze

River flood in China. The news of disaster filled the media, but nothing was said by political leaders or news reporters about the climate-change connection."[7]

In both the story of Ice and the Sea Otter Woman and the story of the Prince and the Frog the violation involves lack of respect for the source or seed of life; in fact, the images—Frog as "womb of regeneration" and the "basket of immortality" that Sea Otter woman carries—are very similar. In the Haida story, however, "the mother's curse" comes from the fire of the Great Mother, the Mountain. At first glance, the connection between Frog and Volcano Woman seems odd. In mythic language, however, the correlation is striking and beautiful. The Frog represents the watery womb of regeneration, the continuation of life. The Mountain, although round and full as Frog, carries Fire in the Belly—the red hot flow of transformation.

Liza Jones

"She wore a labret in her lower lip and held in her hand a cane topped with the picture of a frog."

CRONE TREKKING IN COYOTE LAND

IN YOUR MUSE:
Respect for the Source

1. Create image cards from the following list (choose the ones that call to you).
"Frog Woman"
"Old Woman"
"Mother/Daughter"
"Carrying the Seed"

2. In your particular art form, go deeper with one of these images.

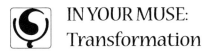

IN YOUR MUSE:
Transformation

1. Create image cards from the following list, choosing the ones that call to you.
"Fire in the Belly"
"The Mother's Cauldron"
"Mid-wife Goddess"

2. A time when you became "Volcano Woman" in response to violation.
   A time when you experienced transformation by Fire.

3. Sketch in words or images "The Wasteland of Loneliness."

Add image cards to your Frog Woman Deck.

"Careless, Indifferent,
Thoughtless, Arrogant..."

One of the most haunting lessons of the Frog Woman story is that the villagers, the adults, are clearly as responsible for the violation as are the boys. They are not paying attention. Busy with their affairs, they do not listen to the boys or to the warnings. They, too, are the "proud ones" who must be destroyed. Still, they are not bad people. In fact, the story is a reminder for "ordinary" people. Mentoring the young is a difficult and continuous task. Most parents will tell you they feel like they fall short of what they, themselves, expect. When there is no strong cultural framework that honors the sacred and supports the child through passages of growth, the task of mentoring becomes even more challenging. What is sometimes required is reinventing meaningful ritual. I call this "making rite."

When my grandson Jeremy was twelve, he went through a difficult time. I listened to my son who had by then been a single parent for ten years, describe Jeremy's attitudes in a voice that broke with frustration and anger. "He's careless, indifferent, thoughtless, arrogant..." The list went on.

"Careless, indifferent, thoughtless, arrogant..." I repeated to myself, thinking it was probably not the right time to mention the list sounded familiar. Hadn't parents, through time, recited this list like a litany? Hadn't I, myself, used these very words?

At twelve Jeremy was the age that boys in some traditional cultures go through an initial rite of passage. But our family was not from a traditional culture, nor did we have such rituals passed down to us. The problem was clear, however. Jeremy needed to be reconnected to the people who cared about him and to the earth. What we did have was a deep family connection to the earth. We decided that Jeremy would come stay with me in the forest for several days. It was clear his father needed a break. And then family and friends, his clan, would gather for a ceremony which we would create to affirm Jeremy and our support of his growth.

Since I had a stretch of time to occupy Jeremy before the family ceremony, I decided to do some "ground" work. Jeremy knew the basic plan: that the family was going to gather to celebrate his being twelve years old—almost a man. "Find a place that feels special to you." I told him the first day. "This will be where we will hold the ceremony. Take your time and be sure it feels like the right place." It didn't take much guessing to know it would be down by the gravel bar on the creek where he loved to play. Later that day, Jeremy led me to a secluded spot on the creek, and we sat on the rocks for awhile talking about the place and watching the filtered light make snakeskin patterns in the water.

The next day I asked Jeremy to spend some time in the place he had chosen to see if he could determine which way was East, and to mark the direction with a special stone. Since he knew where the sun came up, he thought that was pretty simple. We talked about the earth symbolism of each of the directions. At Wanderland, the ocean is our West; the mountain, Onion Peak, headwaters of our creek, is to the North; and the sunny lands of California to the South. By the end of the day, Jeremy had a circle with the four directions marked by stones, and a basic sense of the symbolism of the "medicine wheel," created by the four directions and the cycle of the seasons. This was a very natural kind of symbolism for him to understand since it came directly from his experience of the earth.

The day before the ceremony we decorated the circle and talked about the association of the directions with the elements: air, fire, water, earth. Jeremy was still following pretty easily and liked the idea of getting the circle ready for the rest of the family to see. At the end of that day I added the names of the animals. We used traditional imagery here: Eagle (East), Coyote (South), Bear (West), Buffalo (North). We talked about their qualities and how each was symbolic of the direction. This was a little harder since Jeremy did not have experience knowing the animals, but I could tell the trickster, Coyote, was his favorite. We hunted wood in the forest and laid the fire in the center of the circle. Then we placed sitting stones around the circle and we were ready.

On the morning of Jeremy's ritual, I asked him to find a special tree near his circle and to spend some time with it, feeling the depth of its roots in the earth, the strength of its trunk against his own body, and how high its branches went. Although we didn't do it at the time, I wish now I had asked him to draw the tree and that we had kept a journal day by day of the images and conversations we had. For the young and the old alike, memory is such an ephemeral thing. At the designated time family and friends gathered at The Forest House. Jeremy led us, drumming, the quarter mile to his special place. I still hold that memory in my heart: family and friends following behind this special twelve year old boy, drumming, singing, chanting, as he took us to the place he had prepared. I did not know, however, the surprises the ritual would bring and the deep stirring it would create in the roots of our family.

 MAKING RITE:
With Children

1. Teach a child earth grounding with the help of a tree. Let them find their special tree. Then have them stand with their back against the tree, imagining roots going down, trunk, branches—until they feel like they are the tree. Have them draw the tree. Show them that they can remember being the tree without standing next to it.

2. Invent a rite of passage or an affirmation ceremony for a child. Start by clarifying the purpose of the ritual. Find symbols for the qualities or experiences you want to honor in the ritual. These may be objects or images. For instance, what are the gifts of womanhood that you would give a young girl? Create an action or sequence of actions that symbolize the purpose of the ritual. For instance, decorated a path with symbolic markers that remind the child of major stages/events in her life from birth to the present. Decorate the last marker as a gateway. Have her clan waiting there, in circle, to give her small gifts that symbolize her uniqueness and power. Use song, drumming, rhythm making. The loving focus of adults who see the child's beauty is the most powerful element.

 PRACTICE:
Teaching Children Respect for Nature

1. In what ways do you teach the young what you hold sacred? Make a list of attitudes toward nature you would like to pass on to the children. Brainstorm with others how to do this. Consider outdoor adventures, stories, ecological education, films, actions (i.e. tree plantings, neighborhood litter cleanup), play, ceremony.

2. Create a "Children in Nature" group and put your ideas into action.

Ancestral Dreaming

"Something is going on with the ancestors," I comment to my daughter as we share our recent dreams over the phone, "since Jeremy's ritual."

It is late October at Wanderland, about a month since my grandson Jeremy's rite of passage. The rains have come and the earth smells sweet with fallen alder leaves. By five in the afternoon, I am shrouded in dusk and drive around the mountain to watch the evening light linger an hour longer over the ocean. We are going down. The falling is coming fast. The lush green is dying back. The earth breathes out cold. We are close to Halloween. In Celtic mythology it is a "between time," a crucial juncture between the seasons. Through the crack in space/time that appears at this juncture, the ancestors come, bringing gifts to their living relations.

West Coal Creek, swollen with the fall rains, has swept the gravel bars clean, leaving on one, a small circle of scattered stones—the remains of Jeremy's medicine wheel. Surrounding it is a larger circle of sitting stones, wet in the rain. My mind fills with the memory of the late summer afternoon when we sat here, in the sunshine by the creek's edge, a circle of family and friends, a clan, gathered to support Jeremy's growing from child to man.

Jeremy sits in the South, across from me. In him I see the child I have loved since the moment he was born; in him, I see the child becoming a man. At times, his father says, he just doesn't care— about anything. Today, Jeremy's face, framed by long, black hair, looks very clean— open. "We are here because we support your growing," I remind Jeremy, "but your root goes deeper still. Many have gone before you

Joe Balden

Stone Circle—West Coal Creek

Stones—West Coal Creek

who give you the gift of life." Then we named those we remembered: generations of grandfathers and grandmothers; my own grandfather, who smelled like the earth he farmed and loved; my mother who had the gift of "making"—warm clothes, quilts, apple pies. The foremothers and forefathers of Jeremy were called into the circle; many of their names Jeremy had never before heard. In that moment by the creek at Wanderland, we were a family tree, rooted deeply in the past and blossoming into the future. Two days after Jeremy's ritual, the ancestral dreaming began.

I am drifting between waking and sleeping. My grandfather is standing near me in the room. He is tall and strong. He wears the familiar blue, striped bib-overalls. He is so real I am surprised to see him; yet I know he is a spirit person. As I cry out my greeting, "Granddad, it is so good to see you," and reach out to hug him, my heart flows into his. Coming into waking, I am still filled with the warmth of our embrace.

"Perhaps it is because of the new path I named *Grandfather Way* that my grandfather has come to me like this," I ponder the next day. The path leads to an ancient stump, reminder of the giant forest that stood here one hundred years ago. When I first came across the stump, I stood a long time watching as faces and shapes emerged and disappeared in the line and shadow of the wood. It was my grandfather who taught me to "see," to see beyond the surface to the magic, in the rock, in the tree. His presence stayed with me through the days that followed my dream until slowly I began to understand something else. "You stand now for Jeremy where I stood for you," he tells me without the words.

My daughter speaks to me of her dream. She walks toward her grandfather's house. It is small and dark. The curtains are closed as they were when he was dying and she is afraid. What is she doing here, she wonders, at the home of this grandparent who never seemed to understand her, never approved of who she was. Still, she pushes open the sliding glass door and enters. The house fills with light and is tall like a cathedral. Her grandfather stands before her, radiant. Reaching out to her, he gives her a gift. And she feels in that moment his love for her and his support for her path.

My older daughter calls from Seattle and leaves a message on the machine. She has had a dream of her grandmother, she says, and can I call her back. "I am in the kitchen of grandma and grandad's house," she says. "I am cooking waffles and I know I am doing it wrong. I am burning them. Smoke fills the house. I know grandma is going to find me doing it wrong. She comes around the corner into the kitchen. But instead of scolding me, we see each other and our hearts open. All of my guilt and fear and frustration fall away in the love that floods between us." My daughter goes on to tell me the new adventures of her first born, now six months old. Her days are filled with mothering.

A strengthening, a healing, is happening in the roots of our family tree since the rite we created "for Jeremy." We wonder at the magic of it and feel its echoes in this place, this remnant of a living rainforest surrounded by clear-cut in the Pacific Coast Range. The roots of my family go six generations into Oregon country. Jeremy's ancestors have been loggers, trappers, hunters, farmers. They have loved Oregon deeply and participated in the destruction of its wilderness. My father lived to see the expanses of forest disappear and the end of the great salmon runs. Jeremy must be taught in schools that such forests and wild life at one time lived.

"Choose an animal from your medicine wheel," I told Jeremy on the day of his ritual, "and ask what it has to teach you." Alone in the forest, Jeremy asked Coyote. But it was not coyote who came. Beyond Jeremy's intending, beyond his choosing, Buffalo appeared. "What you care for will give back to you," the Buffalo said.

A few weeks later, Jeremy and I are having dinner together in a Portland restaurant. "It's almost Halloween. What are you going to be?" I ask. Halloween, I know, is one of his favorite holidays. "I'm just going to be ugly," he replies, reminding me once more of the startling mixture of wisdom and contrariness that he is at 12. We have spent the dinner hour in animated discussion. Jeremy has, in the last week, experienced his first shamanic journey. His face is full of excitement. Something new and full of wonder has opened in him. "I went to Wanderland," he tells me, "to my circle. The Buffalo came but turned and walked North, upstream. Then a big Elk appeared. The Elk told me—'you are doing well.' "

"The Elk is Grandfather of the place," I reply, looking at Jeremy. His face is full of Beauty.

I would not want to leave the impression that this one ritual solved all Jeremy's problems or those of his family. Growing is, after all, continually new as are the challenges. Jeremy had his 16th birthday in the year 2000. Tall and slim, his body toned like an acrobat, he is a rock climber. He dreams of buying a van after high school and traveling across the country with his dog, Charlie. On his adventure, he would climb the most difficult places he could find. "Anything to escape *those two!*" he says. His father has fallen in love and remarried. In talking with him recently about Jeremy, I heard the words, "He's arrogant, thoughtless, careless... ."

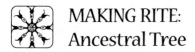 MAKING RITE:
Ancestral Tree

Create a ceremony that deepens a child's connection to his or her ancestors. Start by collecting photos and memories of the ancestors. Spend some time drawing a familty tree with the child. Make or collect things that are symbolic of the gifts each ancestor brings. For example, "the gift of good cooking," "the gift of laughter," "the gift of loving nature," "love of family"...

Create a game or a ritual of ancestral gift giving. For instance, actually decorate a tree with the symbols; or put them around the house in appropriate places and let the child find them; or let the child draw the gifts from a pot and then match them to the ancestor (color coding gift with name of ancestor works).

To Stand in Awe of the Deity

I live in the foothills of a magic mountain. It is actually a volcanic ridge, a sinuous spine of rocky peaks with a face looking out over the ocean. The mountain is a nightmare to the highway department because it has a habit of dropping large rocks on Highway 101. If you have heard thunder shake the mountain, you know why the Native People named it Neah-kah-nie, "Where the Spirits Walk." People who spend time here in the forest dream deeply and sometimes speak of hearing unusual sounds—drumming, singing, voices talking above the murmuring of creek waters.

I have lived with the mountain now for ten years. I have heard the sounds. I have felt the earth move beneath me as I sat in meditation. Only once, however, have I heard the mountain roar—Was it thunder? Was it an explosion? Or was it the footstep of the gods? I still do not know.

I had just sat down to relax in the late afternoon sun after a day of working in the forest. I didn't know if my exhaustion was from the work, or from the noise of logging that had started at dawn. Apparently they had finished for the day. I breathed in the silence and slowly realized how much my body had been braced against the sounds—the insistent whining of chain saws, the trees cracking, the thud of large bodies against the earth. Now, in the quiet, I listened to the forest—wind, water, bird songs. And noticed Luna, my malamute friend, walking toward me with that sick smile that means she is **very** worried.

Then the mountain shook with an explosion so loud that I jumped from my chair. I waited for what was to follow. Nothing. Only the sounds of the forest. "It didn't happen," I tried to tell myself. But I knew it had and it was too big to ignore. "Where did Luna go?" I wondered as I walked quickly down the hill to my daughter's camp by the creek. She was standing outside her tent, dazed.

"What happened?" she asked. "I was napping; then there was an explosion, and Luna was trying to get me up and out of the tent. If I hadn't gotten out, she would have ripped the tent apart." We looked at each other in bewilderment.

"Maybe we should go to town and see what people are saying," I said. We started walking back up the hill to the car. Half way there, I stopped. "I can't do it," I said. "I need to stay here." We turned around and walked the other direction, as if compelled, to the outer boundary of this forest I call Wanderland. Suddenly, we were there—looking into the new clearcut. Blue sky, just blue sky, and fallen trees. "Maybe it will become a meadow," my daughter said hopefully. I stood in shock—my heart pounding. "Breathe, just breathe," I kept reminding myself. The forest that had been there this morning was gone.

All summer I had lived in tension with a neighbor whose only access to his land is a narrow rock lane across the hillside that is Wanderland. "The lane must be widened for the log trucks," he told me. "You cannot cut trees along the lane without my permission," I replied. His answer came at dawn, the morning of the plant medicine workshop. I was awakened by the sound of chain saws, dogs barking, motors. Then quiet. My neighbor had come and gone. The lower lane was littered with smashed and broken trees, most of them alder and elderberry. A huge old elderberry, mossgrown and covered with ferns, lay fallen in the creek; others were battered and tossed along the steep bank.

I remember the plant workshop of that weekend through a veil of shock. A few words, however, echoed in my mind long after: "Elderberry is said to be sacred to the elders. Red ones, like these, are poisonous, however," the teacher remarked as she moved quickly on to the next plant. "A plant sacred to the Elders must carry powerful medicine," I thought. That night, I sat by the creekside drumming, drumming out my rage, drumming out my grief, singing to the forest, singing to the elders of this place, singing to the Elderberry trees.

In the following weeks, I learned very rapidly about Elder's gifts and medicine. Friends gave me articles and unusual books appeared. I learned not only that elk do eat Elderberry, but that Native People let the animals show them what plants were edible and medicinal. Elder's name appears to come from "aeld" (fire) because the dead outer branches are hollow and can be used as fire blowers. Native People also used them to make flutes. Because Elderberry offered so many gifts, it was thought to house the spirit of the forest. If you cut or harmed an Elderberry tree without asking permission of the "witch" who lived in the tree, you would have bad luck. This, of course, is superstition.

The word, theologians tell us, comes from the Latin root *supersisto*, "to stand in terror of the Deity." Magic is often marked by a sequence of synchronistic events, so striking that we have the feeling they *must* mean something, even though often we are not sure what. So it was on the day the mountain roared. Was it an explosion? Was it thunder? Was it the roar of the gods? I do not know. I only know it struck at the heart of my emotion and left me in awe

Meanwhile, my neighbor and I walked the lane together, talking about what was needed, tree by tree. Feelings were raw. Our needs were different, and so was our way of seeing. We did not even have a mutual agreement about our rights. We knew, however, that we could not just leave, nor could we afford to be enemies. We lived here together, side by side. And so we tried to work it out, preparing the way for the log trucks to pass through. Something had been lost between us, however, that was not easily regained—a trust, a comfortable friendliness.

I now look back at this episode through five years. I remember the pain I felt losing something I cared about, the surrender to what I could not prevent—and the anger that raged through me. And even more clearly, I remember the sadness of the severed relationship with my neighbor. We could not understand each other. I missed the friendly smile and wave as they passed through. I missed the moments of easy chatting, leaning out the windows of our cars as we paused a moment in our passing. It was a high price and it took years to even begin to heal. We had come to our interaction with different needs and different ways of seeing, and instead of seeking ways to talk it through and reach agreement, we quickly polarized—each convinced we were right. Both of us were left feeling hurt and angry.

I have come to understand more in recent years how the fire of my passion can fuel misunderstanding as well as powerful action. Unfortunately, it is a tempering that usually comes after the fact when I begin to wonder, "What did I do wrong?" "How could I have done better than this?" The Greeks recognized this as a common human experience by creating a god called Epimetheus, "after thought." It is a reflective gift that Coyote lacks!

How can we communicate well during disagreements? For me, the first step is to breathe through and process the anger before I speak—not to let it drive the communication. For anger fuels anger, and almost always leads to more extreme polarization. Drumming, dancing, free writing, meditating, breathing, voicing in a safe place—all of these help me work through to a place where I can again hear the other person. Certainly, calling on a mediator is a practical way to keep relationship when communication breaks down. A mediator can also help you see through the other's eyes when you are more inclined to create an enemy than to empathize. One of the best self-help books I have read on how to find common ground in the face of conflict is Joanna Macy's *Despair and Empowerment in the Nuclear Age* .

In the case of my neighbor and me, it took a peacock to break the ice between us. Several years had gone by when the peacock just showed up in my garden one day. You can imagine my astonishment, when a six foot iridescent bird strutted around the corner of my car and looked me in the eye. I was on my way to a meeting and hadn't a clue what to do about this strange visitor, so I just left—thinking surely the bird would be gone when I returned, if it wasn't an hallucination to start with! When I returned after a few hours, the peacock stood within several feet of my sleeping Malamute, Luna, eyeing her curiously. My arrival, however, sent Luna into action and the peacock into a nearby tree.

By evening, I had discovered that the peacock, who had been wandering around in the forest for a week before it found his way to my garden, actually belonged to my neighbor. Then began the many adventures of trying to herd this contrary bird back down the road to his home. We had to surrender more than once. The bird would go part way, and then, suddenly head back up the bank and disappear into the forest. One morning, as I was driving down the driveway, I found him strutting in front of some recycled windows admiring his reflection.

The peacock escapade went on for several days before we finally succeeded in getting him back to his home. Sometimes there is nothing so healing as working together toward a common goal—and the frustrations, ingenuity, and laughter that it engenders. The peacock gave us that gift. We became people again and neighbors. A few weeks later, I found a bouquet of peacock feathers left near the Wanderland sign.

My mythic self enjoys that the peacock was once a bird of the goddess, for the "eyes" on its tail feathers were a reflection of Her many-eyed wisdom, Her clarity of vision. Certainly we are in need of such a totem for we live in a time of very strong passions and opinions concerning the balance between individual right and environmental concern. One of the gifts of community based Watershed Councils has been to provide a training ground for listening and empathizing with many different views—without going into a rage—and then, hopefully, to come to some understanding of a common goal that forms the basis for action.

For me, the challenge of such councils is not to lose my voice, my courage to speak, even when the majority do not agree with me—and to speak in a way that is clear and forceful, but does not polarize. Many times, I have to surrender to the fact that what I want is not going to happen—at least not in the immediate future. That, however, does not make it less important to speak. When it feels hopeless and discouraging, I remind myself of John Seed's observation—the earth, the forests, the animals, the waters do not have voices to speak. We must be their voices. Surely, our common human goal is to live together in harmony on the earth—without destroying it.

 IN YOUR MUSE:
Standing in Awe

"A moment when you "stood in awe of the Deity," or had no explanation for an event.

 IN YOUR MUSE:
Balancing Passion and Surrender

1. Tempering: What situations has your passion created? Take a situation that has stayed strong in your memory. Honor the god Epimetheus by making a list of "after thoughts." What did the situation teach you?

2. A time you surrendered to something you could not prevent. Freewrite the frustration, the anger. What were the lessons that emerged? The gifts?

The Magic Bowl

"Where do I go from here?" I asked myself, having landed from several days of writing in an empty space, totally blocked. I was stuck, uninspired, and I had a whole evening left to work. "What now?" My Harpies, sensing the void, began to close in "Why bother? Who cares? You've got yourself in a ridiculous position—caught between logic and superstition. Give it up." I have an especially sharp inner critic I call "Rick" who's a composite of voices from my past: a brilliant analytical brother who would simply give me that disdainful look that meant "how could you be so stupid"? or dismiss my thoughts with one final word—"nonsense"; years in Academia, where others would simply point out that's not "logical" or there's no "proof" of that, apparently having never experienced anything similar themselves. Or worst possible fate: "You're too emotional! What are you a mystic or something?" So I have these conversations with Rick, especially in times of self doubt:

"You're trying to tell me you think nature has emotions? Ridiculous!"

"What I am saying is that nature is highly intelligent and sensitive, responds to our actions."

"But you are saying there are nature *spirits*. That's nonsense! It's superstitious, sentimental, emotional..."

"Yes, I *am* saying spirit is in nature and appears in many ways, that it speaks to us if we listen. Rick—just shove off! I've got work to do."

I start browsing books, filling my mind with images (instead of Rick). I look through the pages of Marija Gimbutus' encyclopedia, *Language of the Goddess,* beautiful bowls engraved with spirals, circles, zigzags. Images of frog that go back to the beginning of human history. "But where do I go next in the writing?" I ask again and decide on a long hot bath and falling asleep to Jennifer Goodenberger's lovely piano composition, "Return." I love the way it washes me in starlight and moonlight and takes me deep into the well of being.

Then I fall into dream. Directly above the head of my bed, in the West corner of my room, is a cauldron filled with radiant light that moves and swirls as if not held by a container at all. When I approach it, I feel a rush of nurturing, a wholeness flow throughout my body. I begin to feel like this is not unusual. It is just there. When I awake, I am still full of the experience, moving slow, in between worlds. Then I realize with a jolt that the ritual bowl I had used for a regeneration ritual and a recent Imbolc retreat was sitting on a table in the West corner of my room, directly beyond the head of my futon. "All right, Rick," I couldn't resist saying to the empty room, "I felt the energy of that bowl in my dream, and it was beautiful beyond words." I knew the next thread of my writing.

Joe Balden

Bowl as cauldron of regeneration

The bowl is about the size of a volleyball and round, even on the bottom. Marked in chalk on one side are the letters A(O). The O has rubbed off over the years. I know nothing of its history before I found it in a small Portland import shop. I have speculated that the AO meant Alpha and Omega—beginning and ending, or that perhaps AO is the name of an ancient goddess of birth and death and rebirth, of "regeneration." For several years now we have used the bowl in women's circles as the cauldron of creation, the womb of the Great Mother. It has within its belly kernels of corn of many colors—the potential, the wishes and dreams of many women.

Last week, in a late winter ritual, the bowl became a musical instrument as I moved my hand through the corn, and played the sound of rain, the sound of change, the sound of moving forces within the womb of creation. Then each woman took handfuls of the seeds to put in her own bowl and we sat in circle playing the bowls and singing the potential of new growth within us. Afterwards, we lay on the floor in meditation, our bowl resting on our belly, and merged with the earth, going deeply. From this deep rest, we felt the stirring and the sprouting begin—new life, pushing through the dark body of the earth. So completely had we become earth that no one wanted to get up. For a few moments, I thought I might have this spring—ten women sprouting on the floor of the main room in the Forest House.

On February 2, I celebrated Imbolc with a circle of women. More popularly known as Candlemas, Imbolc is the first of the eight cross-quarter Holy Days, the Celtic New Year. I like to use the older Celtic name because it reminds me of the quickening of life "in belly" that this seasonal holy day honors. I placed the bowl on the center altar, where it symbolized the "cauldron of regeneration," and around it placed many large smooth stones from a nearby beach, reminding us of the power of water in honing our essential selves. Our ritual, over the weekend, was to be focused with the elements of water and fire. Water, as the abundant spring rains drench the rainforest; water in the sounds of the creeks and the dripping of the trees; water, that washes us clean of the old and plumps the seeds of new sprouting. Fire, in the increasing light of lengthening days; fire, in the slow warming of the earth; fire, in the life spark that kindles and begins to grow.

We started with the "spark," the impulse. "What do I need? What do I want? What do I desire?" we asked ourselves, and wrote freely without censorship in our journals. Then without talking about it, we walked the quarter mile to the creek and sat, listening to the waters, letting go until the voices of the creek filled us, and we were the sound of water. "Februa," we were reminded, means purification. We soaked in a hot tub filled with spring water. Later in the day, we quietly, each in our own time, tended the spark. Looking at each of our needs/wants/desires, we let go to the stream, and said, "I let go of ____;" what I really want is ____," and then we observed the changes. "Most of mine," one woman commented, "grew less specific, broader."

In the evening, we planned a ritual drama celebrating the story of Brighida, Celtic Triune Goddess of Creativity. Brighida is associated with all four elements; in fact, she is the whole cauldron of creative muses. She is the excitement of new ideas, of inspiration, words, poetry; She is the joy of creative fire, the fire that transforms water into tea, clay into pots, hearth into home; She is the healing waters of purification, renewal, and life; She is ingenuity, making and shaping things with our hands: tools, medicines, structures that give form to our creativity. Brighida's story divides easily into four "scenes." These, we created improvisationally with costumes (scarves, capes, hats...) movement, and sound.

Scene One: The Crone Chorus

The Story Teller: *In the beginning, at the very first dawning, when light is first being birthed from the womb of darkness, nine crones, midwives of the Goddess Brighida, sing and chant her birthing song.*

The women are dressed in black, the chant rises and breaks into song, and deepens and then rises again. Voices fill the room as night gives birth to day, as winter gives birth to spring, as we give birth—shedding the old, radiant with light.

Scene Two: The Fire Dance

The Story Teller: *When the Goddess Brighida was born , a column of fire flamed from her head to the heavens like a fountain. She was a young goddess, full of laughter, full of playfulness. She reached up and took a handful of that fire and threw it to the earth. She could see its many possibilities and she began to dance the fire. She became fire dancing.*

The women, holding brightly colored scarves, swirl around in the room, playing dancing, laughing.

Scene Three: The Making

The Story Teller: *The Goddess Brighida found joy in making things. She discovered that from fire and water she could create something totally new. She made teas, and medicines, and soups. She discovered shaping and firing bricks and pots. She loved to watch the sparks fly from the metal she crafted into tools. She loved the feel of tools in her hands.*

The women sit in circle around the central altar. They are using the stones from the altar, pounding them against each other as tools. They are enjoying the movement of their hands, keeping rhythmic time. The sound of stones and hands grows larger; the women begin to sway and move with the sound until they are joined as one, a tribe of women, making, singing, creating.

Scene Four: The Healing Waters

The Story Teller: *Word of Brighida's magic traveled far across the land. Stories told of a sacred well, where the healing waters of the Mother spiraled deeply to the center of the earth, and then rose again, continuously renewing. One day, two sisters came, seeking the cleansing waters and Brighida's healing hands. The sisters were dark with disease, their bodies shriveled and ugly. Brighida, taking the first sister to the well, saw the beauty of her spirit as the waters washed her clean and the sores vanished from her skin. The woman, newly whole, rejoiced.*

"Now, wash your sister in the well and see her whole," Brighida told the woman. But the sister was repelled by the other. She saw only the darkness. She saw only the disease. "No," she said, "I cannot." "Then you, yourself, are not healed," Brighida told her, as the darkness and the sores reappeared over her body. "You will find your healing in your heart," Brighida told her, touching her heart with her hand. Then she took the second sister and washed her clean in the well until the radiance shown from her like a newly born star. And the first sister journeyed far into the depths of her own heart until her heart opened, merged with the radiant heart of the Mother, and she was transformed by the waters of compassion.

The women, in twos, fill a bowl with water from a large cauldron of spring water at the West altar. They sit across from each other and in turn cleanse each other with the water: "I see your beauty; I see your wholeness; I see in you—goddess," they repeat, until they see clearly the beauty of the other.

Walking single file into the star-lit night, the women chant, "She is quickening; she is quickening. I feel her quickening." When they reach the spring fed pond, they each light a candle to the quickening of life within the earth and within themselves. The light from the candles dances around the pond as the women sing songs to the earth and to the night. Late into the night, the candlelight can still be seen from the Forest House, flickering like stars in the dark forest.

"I can see, Rick, that you've left the room altogether. I did want to tell you one more thing." Thomas Moore speaks of *seeing* the spirit of the Divine in Joan Hanley's art: "She makes images that invite passing spirits to take notice and often take up residence," [8] he says. Ritual uses images in the same way, to attract and "hold" the Divine so we can experiece it. In this way, the veil drops from between the worlds of "magic" and "reality." I asked to feel the cauldron of regeneration within my body and that is what my dream experience—stirred by the ritual, stirred by Frog Mother—brought to me.

 ## IN YOUR MUSE

1. Create image cards from the story of Brighida. In your particular art form, go deeper with one of the cards.

3. Write a dialogue between you and one of your frequent self critics.

2. Add image cards to Frog Woman Deck.

 ## MAKING RITE:
Cauldron of Creation

1. **Clarifying Desire:** Start with the "spark," the impulse. Brainstorm without censoring, "What do I need? What do I want? What do I desire?" Use water, if possible a creek or the ocean (if not a bowl of water) to let go of each desire and be washed clean. Then, in your own time, go back over your list with the lead: "I let go of...;" "what I really want is..." and observe the changes.

2. **In circle create a "Cauldron of Creation" ritual** using bowls containing kernels of corn as musical instruments to stimulate the birthing of the creative self. (see description in "The Magic Bowl")

3. **In circle create a cleansing ritual** using bowls filled with fresh spring water. Sit in twos across from each other and in turn cleanse each other with the water repeating: "I see your beauty; I see your wholeness; I see in you—goddess," until you see clearly the beauty of the other.

4. **Create a ritual drama** by dividing a myth into scenes and enacting the archetypes, using costumes, masks, instruments, movement.

Rain and water lines enclose eggs marked with X's, representing
their inherent regenerative energy. Ukraine, 3900 B.C.E.

Where is the Edge?

I am walking on the edge of the Mother's heart—
a spring fed pond at the top of Mt. Hebo.
The water moss glows golden green,
and crunches beneath my feet
as they sink four inches
down and come back dry.
I am drawn closer
but there's no way to tell
where earth becomes water
where pond becomes moving sky.
Then the vibration around me grows
to a golden hum
and I begin to worry about the edge
for there's no way to distinguish
between insects, and color, and me.

gwendolyn

WILD CARDS

Playing with the FROG WOMAN DECK.

You have now completed your Frog Woman Deck of image cards. The images of this deck reflect the regenerative powers within you—and your attitudes toward the earth and the sacredness of life. Shuffle the deck and pull four cards, a fifth if you choose. Arrange the cards in any way you desire: in a sequence, a circle, a collage...freewrite the story of the cards. Follow your Muse in going deeper.

In Circle

1. If you are working with a circle, shuffle everyone's images together and use them like a deck of cards, passing them around for everyone to choose from until they are gone. Follow the same process of laying them out in sequence and telling or sketching their story. You can also invent rules. A "discard" pile might be interesting where you can get rid of one but must take another. Play around.

2. In a circle, play around with the images through aspecting and improvisational drama. Each choose an image. Get into the energy—dress like it, move like it, sound like it. A group of eight or so doing this with different aspects at once is wildly energizing! Afterwards, pass the talking stick or write in your journal. What did the experience feel like in your body?

STORY FOUR

Liza Jones

SPIDER WOMAN AND THE MAKING OF WORLDS

Out of her body she pushed
silver thread, light, air
and carried it carefully on the dark, flying
where nothing moved.
Out of her body she extruded
shining wire, life, and wove the light
on the void

PAULA GUNN ALLEN
(FROM GRANDMOTHER, 1997)

Tales of Mathilda

A spider has made her home at my hearth. I first noticed her at a women's circle in September. She hung from the broom that leans against the fireplace in the main room of The Forest House. That evening we watched her munching casually on a flying termite. There she stayed—no problem. Until the next weekend when I had a group coming to stay at Wanderland. I set up sleeping areas for ten people—one almost at face level with Spider.

"It won't work," I thought, even if the group is called "Nature Connect." Besides, she is BIG and what if she bites. I picked up the broom and headed for the door—but she was far faster than me. She leaped—and disappeared, I knew not where. "Oh well," I thought, "maybe she will behave, and not make herself too noticeable."

Moments before the group arrived, I walked through the main room and saw her clearly outlined—black against the ceiling white. "Oh well," I thought. "She stays." I pointed her out as the house spider when I walked the group through. One man commented, "Women seem to like spiders." "I know some who are terrified of spiders," I thought. Later, I wondered if she was the reason they all chose to sleep upstairs. But there she stayed on the ceiling, little noticed as weeks passed by.

Now, almost six weeks later as Halloween approaches, she has become more bold. She sits at the center of a perfect circular web in a window of the main room. Now this is not a small web, but at least a 12 inch disk, delicately woven. "It's almost Halloween," I think, "how could I possibly..." Later on, I notice that I have started thinking of her by name. I call her Mathilda.

In early November, The Forest House was filled with people who had come for an "Art Happening" that included art, readings, and music provided by "The Full Moon Drummers"—all focused on the theme "Love of Place." Just as the drummers began to really get into their rhythm, Mathilda the Spider dropped down on a single thread and hovered in mid-air, right in front of the lead drummer—becoming front row audience on the plushest of air cushions, hung from who-knows-where above. "Is this the spider you've been writing about?" Bob, the drummer, asked, looking her square in the eye. When it was my turn to read, it seemed obvious that her story, The Tale of Mathilda, was expected. Afterwards, she took a kind of bow, midway—and went back to sit on the ceiling—this time directly above my friend Lucy's head.

"I think she's getting bigger," I said, looking at the dark black shadow on the ceiling. Then someone from the back of the room quipped, "What happened to Lucy?" We all laughed—for a moment seeing Lucy invisible and Mathilda's belly growing larger. Later, Lucy said, "She was right above me the whole time, but she never did drop down on me." Lucy, it seems, has passed fear of spiders.

Liza Jones

Shortly after her on-stage appearance, Mathilda disappeared. I could find her nowhere for a couple of weeks. And then, one night I saw her—or someone who looked very much like her—sitting on the wall, just six inches from where *I* sat taking a bath. It was an odd sensation feeling at once so large and so vulnerable. I have read that only a very few spiders have bites poisonous to humans, and as far as I know, they do not inhabit this place; still, it took a moment to relax into the warm water and trust this spider spectator so close to my inner world.

"I know of your spinning, Arachnid, Old One," I comment to her, hoping conversation will make me feel less exposed. "You have the forest spun in webs already. And I have heard that this spinning of yours, this making of worlds, goes back to the beginning of time." Spider sat silent, simply regarding me.

STORY FOUR

Spider Woman and the Making of Worlds

In the beginning, say the Hopi, there *was* no beginning, no end, no time, no space. There was immeasurable void, containing everything, all possibilities—containing even Time, Shape, and Life. This was the womb of the Infinite that the Hindus call the goddess Adita whose very name means "abundance," "creative power."

Dream began to stir in that infinite night. In the void, shapes began to form. Or did the Dreamer, Taiowa, dream the void as well as the dream? For in the time of becoming, the two were the same. In that dreaming the Infinite conceived the finite. The "first power and instrument" of creation, the Sun (Sotuknang) was born, taking the form of a person.

It was Sotuknang, as the instrument of Taiowa, who gave form to the dream by shaping nine universes and setting them in harmonious movement in space. Then he created the waters so that the worlds were part water and part earth and set the air swirling into large currents and patterns around the universes. Taiowa and Sotuknang looked at the universes moving in beauty and harmony, and they were pleased. As in Taiowa's dreaming, seven of the universes were for the unfolding of life; the other two were the home of the Infinite—Taiowa and Sotuknang.

Sotuknang then went to the universe wherein was to be the first world, Tokpela. From that universe, Sotuknang created Kokyangwuti, Spider Woman. Her body was shaped like the infinity sign in an 8, and she bore, as well, a reminder of the sun, the many spoked wheel, for she, too, was instrument of the Creator's Dream. This was in the time of the very first dawn when a deep purple light spread throughout creation. Spider Woman awoke and looked around her as if just waking from deep dream. "Where am I? Why am I here?" she asked.

"Look about you," said Sotuknang. "The universes are beautiful. There is shape and substance, direction and time, beginning and end. But there is no life. No joyful sound. No joyful movement. You have been given the power to help create this life. You have been given the knowledge, wisdom, and love to bless all beings you create. That is why you are here."

Spider Woman looked out at the silent, empty, earth. And in the deep purple light of the first dawn, she began to sing. She spun a line from East to West. She spun a line from North to South. Then she sat in the center of these lines she had cast to the four horizons, and she sang in a voice that was exceptionally deep and sweet. She sang the songs of knowledge, wisdom, and love.

And in that moment, she took some earth in her hands and moistened it with spittle. She shaped two beings, and wrapped them in the silver white cloak of creative wisdom that floated web-like around her, the very emanations of her song. She sang to them. Over and over, she sang The Creation Song:

> *The song resounds back from our Creator with joy/ and we of the earth repeat it to our Creator/ At the appearing of the yellow light/ Repeats and repeats again the joyful echo/ Sounds and resounds for times to come.*

When she uncovered them, the twins sat up as if awaking from a dream and asked: "Where are we? Why are we here?" To the one on the right, Spider Woman gave the name of Poqanghoya. "You are to help keep this world in order," she told him, "by putting your hands on it and making it solid. Solidify the higher reaches into great mountains. Make the lower reaches firm but still pliable enough to be used by those beings who would live on it and call it mother." And so Poqanghoya traveled around the earth, shaping the mountains and the valleys, the plains and the deserts.

To the twin of the left, Spider Woman gave the name Palongawhoya. "You will be called echo," she said. "You will help keep this world in order when life is upon it. Travel around the world and send out sound so that it echoes throughout the land." As Palongawhoya traveled throughout the earth sounding out his call, all the vibratory centers along the earth's axis from pole to pole resounded. The whole earth trembled. The universe quivered in tune.

Listening to the song of the universe, Sotuknang said to Taiowa, "This is your voice, Everything is tuned to your sound." Thus, the whole world, and the universe as well, became an instrument of sound, and the sound became an instrument for carrying messages of praise to the Creator.

Spider Woman then took earth in her hands and created the trees, bushes, plants, flowers, and all kinds of seed and nut bearers to clothe the land. On their leaves she left her imprint, spokes radiating out from the center. She gave each plant a life and a name. In the same way from the body of the earth, she created the birds and animals. And again she wrapped each form in her silver substance cape, singing the songs of creation. Life multiplied and spread to cover the earth. Throughout creation, the voice of the creator was heard in the sound of wind and water, the song of birds, and the cry of animals. Spider Woman saw beauty and power working through all creation.

Once more, Spider Woman felt a stirring and the dream of the Creator flowed through her—the sound of laughter, of singing, of dancing and joy. Again she reached into the body of the earth, and she shaped humans in the four colors, yellow, red, white, and black. She covered them with her magic cloak of creative wisdom and she sang over them, repeating again and again, The Creation Song:

> *The dark purple light rises in the north/ A yellow light rises in the east./ Then we of the flowers of the earth come forth/ To receive a long life of joy/ We call ourselves the Butterfly Maidens.*

When Spider Woman uncovered the forms, they came to life and began to awaken. But there was still a soft spot on their heads and a dampness on their forehead. This was the Time of the Yellow Light, when the Breath of Life entered man. Spider Woman sang to them The Creation Song:

> *Both male and female make their prayers to the east/ Make the respectful sign to the Sun our Creator/ The sounds of bells ring through the air/ Making a joyful sound throughout the land/ Their joyful echo resounding everywhere.*

Then the sun appeared above the horizon, drying the newborn dampness from their foreheads and hardening the soft spot on their heads. This was the time known as the Time of the Red Light, when humans, fully formed, faced their Creator. And Spider Woman sang; still she sang The Creation Song:

> *The perfect one laid out the perfect plan/ And gave to us a long span of life/ Creating song to implant joy in life/ On this path of happiness, we the Butterfly Maidens/ Carry out his wishes by greeting our Father Sun.*

"That is the sun," Spider Woman told them as their hearts opened to receive the radiant love. "You are meeting your Creator for the first time." All around them, they heard the song:

> *The song resounds back from our Creator with joy/ And we of the earth repeat it to our Creator/ At the appearing of the yellow light/ Repeats and repeats again the joyful echo/ Sounds and resounds for times to come.*

"Always remember to respect the Creator," Sotuknang told them. "May you never forget wisdom, harmony and respect."

As Spider Woman sang The Creation Song to the first people in her deep, sweet voice, the vibratory centers up and down their spines opened and resounded to the Creator. Thus, the living bodies of the people and the living body of the earth were tuned to each other. All creation was woven and connected in a vibratory web. There was no separation in the First World, no fear between the people and the animals. Even though the people spoke different languages, they spoke the same language telepathically through the doorway at the top of their heads. In this way, the people and the animals also understood each other.

"Always remember the time of the three lights," Spider Woman told them, " the time of the three phases of your Creation. The dark purple is the great mystery of creation; the yellow is the first breath of life, and the red is the warmth of love." As the people spread out over the earth in the time of the first world, Spider Woman went with them, always reminding them by her form, by her webs, of their connection to each other and to the Creator. And when they looked at the sun, they saw the face through which looked Taiowa, their Creator.

But gradually people began to forget the teachings of Sotuknang and Spider Woman. There came among them one called the Talker. The more he kept talking, the more he convinced them of their differences—in appearance, in color, in speech, in beliefs. The animals pulled away from the people. "The guardian spirit of the animals laid his hands on their hind legs just below the tail, making them become wild and scatter from the people in fear." In the same way, people began to divide and pull away from each other. All but a few forgot

Sun and spider symbols on pre-historic Hopi pottery.

their connection to the Creator. Those who remembered were ridiculed and scorned, and so they sang the songs quietly, within their hearts, but never stopped singing. The thread ran out on the First World. Sotuknang came like a mighty wind and showed the few who had remembered how to survive in the belly of the earth until it was time to begin again. And the First World was destroyed by fire.

Twice more, Spider Woman sang out the Creator's dream, weaving worlds of harmony, love, and joy. And twice again, the people forgot their connection with the creator and with each other. They became greedy, consumed by their wanting. They built big cities and fought wars. No joyous songs came from the earth. Twice more, the thread was cut and the worlds destroyed to start again. We are now in the Fourth World, say the Hopi. The Fourth World is "not all beautiful and easy like the previous ones. It has height and depth, heat and cold, beauty and barrenness." It has everything to choose from. The choices the people make will determine whether this time they carry out the plan of Creation or whether this world must, in time, be destroyed too. [1]

Doorways Into The Story

Stories are much like mirrors. They reflect back both personal and cultural images. Because of this, different people will see different things in a story. What they see is almost always what is relevant to them, what the story is teaching them. To insist on one meaning violates the magic of a story, the aliveness, which grows and unfolds within the psyche. If you let them, the stories that are particularly relevant to you will attract you; in a sense, the story you need will find *you*. This is also why different stories will inhabit your consciousness at different times in your life. And why sometimes you feel the need for a new story.

If you by-pass analysis and enter a story through the images that stay in your consciousness after hearing it, you are more likely to discover what it is telling *you*. I call these images "doorways" into the story. Enter them gently without pushing too hard or demanding too much, and you will often discover that they unfold in ways that surprise you and offer you totally new insights. The doorway pages of this book offer you the space to enter the story in your own way before being influenced by my mythical musings.

Take a moment now to dwell with the images that stay with you from the story. There is no need to look back at the story or puzzle about it. You already know.

Finding the images:

1. Jot down the main images you remember from the story. Circle the three or four that attract you the most. Consider these your "doorways" into the story.

2. First give each image its own space by sketching it, one to a "doorway." ("Sketching" can be done abstractly with color or symbol as well as representationally).

3. If one of the images attracts you more than the others, focus on that one. Dwell with the image. Remember that the more attention you give an image, the more likely it is to unfold, but don't try to "figure it out."

Looking at the other side of the doorway:

1. After you have spent time dwelling with the image, create the back side of the card by decorating it with symbols or a design that reflects the "teachings" this image has for you.

2. Add image cards to your deck that reflect the teachings of the story.

2. Write an initiation story about passing through one of the doorways . (An initiation story involves going into new territory and the lessons learned.)

Ways to go more deeply with an image:

1. Make a card for the image and put it in a special place. Meditate or dwell with the image. Dream with it.

2. As you look at the image, freewrite your feelings and associations.

3. Give the image a title.

4. See it as an illustration in a book and write the story that goes with it.

5. Look at it as a Tarot card and write a description of its meaning.

6. If you decide to work with all three images, try giving each a title—as a Tarot Card or a chapter in a book might be titled.

7. Arrange the cards in any way that pleases you and tell the story they inspire.

In Circle

1. If you are working with a circle, shuffle everyone's images together and use them like a deck of cards, passing them around for everyone to choose from until they are gone. Follow the same process of laying them out in sequence. You can also invent rules. A "discard" pile might be interesting, where you can get rid of one but must take another.

2. In a circle, play around with the images through improvisational drama. Each choose an image. Get into the energy—dress like it, move like it, sound like it. A group of eight or so doing this with different aspects at once is wildly energizing!

Creating your Spider Woman Deck

Add additional image cards as you finish readings and exercises of this chapter. Follow the reflective lead—what images stay in your mind?

Re-membering the Great Mystery

In astrophysics we meet staggering aspects of time; we can, for instance, look backwards in time, to see the light of stars that have long since disappeared. The universe is in ceaseless motion; rotating clouds of hydrogen gas contract to form stars which continue to rotate, ejecting material into space. Eventually after millions of years, when most of the fuel is used up, the star expands and then contracts again into the final gravitational collapse. This collapse may turn into a black hole, where there is nothing more observable left, including time. Whether the universe has a beginning and end, or moves in cycles of expansion and collapse, or remains in a steady state in which matter is continually created anew, is still a matter of controversy...

MARIE-LOUISE VON FRANZ [2]

On an August evening shortly after I bought Wanderland, some of my family and friends gathered to celebrate the forest. At that time it was, of course, totally forest—no buildings, no indoor facilities, no lights—except for the filtered starlight and moonlight through the trees. We gathered around a small fire, talking, laughing, telling stories. Somewhere into the evening when the darkness had come full, my grandson Jeremy, who was then about five, demanded the bathroom. His dad explained that they would hike out into the woods together and find a spot, and the two disappeared into the dark for what seemed a very long time. Then we heard a five-year-old voice yelling excitedly, "Magic is real! Magic is *real!*" and spirals of sparks moved through the darkness towards us as Jeremy emerged, waving what looked, indeed, like a magic wand. This was our first glimpse of the phosphorescence the forest creates as decay, moisture, and time take wood back to bare bones. To experience this for the first time through the eyes of a child was a special gift of the forest on that night.

Walking the forest in the daytime, you sometimes see a piece of this wood kicking out from the surface of the soil—an interestingly shaped green stick, decayed to its solid core. People often bring a piece back from their walks, asking "What *is* this?" even though it only glows at certain times of the year and, of course, only at night. Although I have never read a scientific explanation of how the forest creates this phenomena, I am sure there is one. What the explanation would leave out is the awesomeness of its happening and the wonder of the sudden discovery in the darkness of the forest. The child, however, is moved deeply by this, not having learned yet to dismiss the wonder through explanation, or with the attitude that wonder *is,* after all, childish.

It is this awe in the presence of mystery, Joseph Campbell says, that lies at the root of mythology; the word, itself, deriving from "mystery." What continually amazes me, however, is how frequently the language of mythology describes with symbols exactly what science explains with facts. The two are often complimentary languages of understanding. Once I get over my amazement at this, I begin to wonder from what senses, from what source of knowing does mythology come? I can only conclude that mythology is a kind of "dream language" similar to personal dreaming. Myths, however, are passed down through time and imprinted by cultures. In this process, symbols are changed; sometimes meanings are changed; sometimes the story, itself, is rewritten. Campbell calls myth a "cultural dream."

This does not mean that all myths are healthy dreams for an individual or a culture. Some myths are nightmares. Some are horror movies. Some reinforce violence and oppression. "Why bother with myths at all?" people ask. Because symbolic language is a very powerful and ancient way of thinking—and because we have a wisdom heritage. The earth is alive with the voices of those who have walked here before us. Many had deep relationships with the earth. Some were dreamers, who understood sacredness and visualized harmony and beauty. Their stories teach us about right-relationship.

It would be nice to have a way to screen out bad mythic dreams. I fantasize something like the "dream catchers" made by Native People—a net like a spider web to catch good dreams and sieve out the bad, for the culture. If I were to make the prototype, it would be from Spider Mother's teachings. It occurs to me that perhaps I have done that already in collecting myths for this book. Often I find myself drawn to the stories of aboriginal people. They take me close to Truth.

Aboriginal peoples are very powerful mythological dreamers because they spiral back to the source for vision. The Australian Aboriginal people do this by literally going back to the place on the earth where they were conceived. This is the place where their spirit was born. Here they can travel the spiral back to origin and become the dreamer. From this place they tell their stories, work their magic, and make their art. This is their place of "emergence." The labyrinthine designs of the Hopi tell a similar story of the journey back to the center of the earth after the end of a "world," and then an emergence: a spiritual rebirth from the old world to the succeeding one.

The Hopi Creation Myth spirals us back before time to Tokpela, "Endless Space," an immeasurable void. It is clear in the myth, however, that the word "void" does not describe an emptiness. Space, "the void," in science as well as in the Hopi story, is a "Great Mystery" filled with the potential of creation. There is physical activity in space: dynamic processes, energy propagating itself. This is why many cultures have symbolized it as "Feminine," and used names like The Matrix, The Eternal Feminine, The Source, Goddess (Aditi, Nut, Neith, Nete). This mystery is sometimes symbolized as a Triangle. The shape of the image is the doorway to the mystery itself which lies within. The triangle (symbolically, the Yoni of the Goddess) then becomes the gateway of creation as life is born from the Mysterious. Thinking this way, then the universe, the planet, and all life was born from a "Great Mystery."

The spiritual force of creation, says Joseph Bruchak, is known by many different names among Native peoples: *manitou, orenda, wakan,* and, among his own people, the Abenaki, as *nwaskw.* Bruchak's Abenaki ancestors describe the creator as *Ktsi Nwaskw,* "Great Mystery."[3] One of the beauties of the Hopi story of creation is the way it reminds us that this undefinable mystery is the Reality behind the names and the actors: "Then he, the Infinite, conceived the finite;" "I have created you, the first power and instrument as a person, to carry out my plan for life..." The people "knew their father (Sotuknang) in two aspects. He was the Sun, the solar god of their universe...Yet his was but the face through which looked Taiowa, their Creator." As Campbell pointed out, the faces are "masks"—metaphors that describe process, energy, spirit.

The formation of Spider Woman, with her eight legs and hour-glass body, is at first startling—so within the finite creature world is she. But this is exactly her power for she is ever present in the lives of the people. In the Creator's Plan, the shape of her body would remind them of infinity (∞). They would look at her webs and see the face of the sun. They would see her weaving, connecting all things, walking the path back to center, and they would remember the Creator's Plan. They would see her pattern, growing, spiraling out from the center, imprinted on nature everywhere, and they would remember the Dreaming at the beginning of time. Hence, nature becomes, in itself, a holographic language—signed by the author and imprinted with the Plan of the Creator.

These are, however, only reminders. In this myth, Spider Woman actually shows the people what action to take, *how* to re-member the connection to source. She, herself, is *born* remembering. When she awakens and first looks out on the silent, empty world, she has already been given the gift of Knowledge, Wisdom, and Love. She is Crone. She knows exactly what to do. She casts her thread to the four directions. She sits in the center and sings her dream. She sits in the center, where the tree of life grows, and sings to the mystery that flows from the four. First she spins sound and vibration, magnetism and form: twins born from the spiraling center. Their energies travel to the four corners and the living world begins: a single organism vibrating in tune with the Creator. Then Spider Woman becomes the midwife goddess. Like the nine old ones in the story of Brighida, she sings the birthing chant. She wraps each being in her cape of wisdom. As midwife she births the spirit into body: from the deep purple light (the mystery) into the gold light (the first breath). Then, their hearts open—love rushes in and love rushes back. They "meet" the Creator.

Remember. Remember the time of the three lights, Spider Woman says. weaving the colors—purple, yellow, and red—weaving them into the very threads of her mother cloak. Remember, this is your way back home. Send out your love on breath, on vibration, on sound. Sound out your love, and it will re-sound back to you. Sound and resound. This is the energy connection; this is the practice Spider Woman repeatedly imprints on the newly born humans. And this is what the Hopi people practice moment by moment of every day. It seems such a simple, commonplace answer that often it is dismissed: "Sending love; giving thanks. Oh yeah, of course." But Spider Woman is not teaching a perfunctory gesture. This is not about words. What she gives to the people is a vibrational connection—sending and receiving—that can be re-membered through sounding, through song, and through prayer.

Even so, the Hopi story tells not only of the teaching but of the forgetting, over and over again. This creation story actually tells the history of *four* beginnings, and three endings. We are now in the fourth world. It is not that Native people did not forget. As Joseph Bruchak points out "The potential for confusion was true for Native people long before the coming of Europeans (though Europeans have raised the art of spiritual confusion to a new level!) That is why the traditional teachings remain so important. They remind human beings how to take care...the right way to behave." [4]

What would it be like to grow up with this teaching, to be part of it from the time of your birth. To be a child, surrounded by family and elders, on the darkest night of the year—a night that stretched out infinitely in stars. What would it be like to listen, year after year, to the story of the Great Mystery and the Dreamer who brought forth creation in beauty, in love, in joy—and whose breath is the very vibration of all life? From your earliest memory to be one with those around you as your voices sound into the dark night sky, repeating and repeating again the joyful echo until that echo filled every day, every moment—and an attitude of joy and thankfulness was your natural state of being.

PRACTICE:
Playing with Echo

"Sound and resound joy" the people are told in the Hopi Creation story. In a special place, where you are free from self consciousness about sound (the ocean or a creek works well) send out your song in words, chant, humming, drumming...The form does not matter; just feel it coming from your heart. Then sit quietly, listen, and receive. Repeat again and again.

IN YOUR MUSE:

1. In the Hopi Creation story, nature's patterns are imprinted by the Creator. Spend time with the earth observing and recording patterns through journaling, sketching, photography.

2. In your particular art form, create an **Archetypal Landscape** from the following suggestions:

"The Void"
"Doorway of Creation" (Focus on the "inside space" of the archetypal symbols triangle or oval)
"The Time of the Purple Light" (awe, mystery)
"The Time of the Gold Light" (awakening, breath)
"The Time of the Red Light" (connection, love)

3. In your particular art form, create an **Archetypal Portrait** from the following suggestions:

"Dreamer"
"Weaver"
"Face of the Sun God/dess

4. Twins: Vibration and Form
Spend time dwelling with your subject—a tree, a flower, a stone, a cloud, a river...Surrender your awareness: follow sound, light, movement. Relax your senses, let go of focus. Let go of definite distinctions in shape and sound. Allow form to shift and change. Stay present in this awareness as long as possible before writing, sketching, painting.

Add images to your Spider Woman Deck.

Notes to Mathilda

You seem to be everywhere lately. It would probably be self centered to think you are so present because I am writing about you, but sometimes I wonder. Yesterday, you hung from a thread by my desk with the flimsiest net spun in front of you and in it one infinitesimal insect who seemed to be entranced, not caught. This I realized when impulse took me and I touched the thread. You ran; the insect flew, and the whole scene vanished in an instant. I was left feeling stupidly large.

And then, this morning, after a night of weaving in and out of spider dreams, I walked out onto the back porch and laughed aloud. During the night, you had spun a cloak over the beaver stick railing. It was a charming touch—the dew sprinkled web sparkled with rainbow light. You really outdid yourself on this one—five feet of web, almost large enough to wear, undulating slightly in the currents of early morning air. It's hard to believe that there wasn't a whole legion of spider feet , in units of 8, tapping away during the night—while I dreamed, tossed and turned, and tried to find the thread into your story. I keep asking you: what is it I am supposed to write? What is your part in this book? And you? You're out there spinning—like I should somehow just get it! It's frustrating to say the least.

One thing is certain. You have made it quite clear that I had a mistaken attitude toward you. For this, I apologize. I admit I thought you would be easy. I have known you for so long and, like an old relationship, I took you for granted. I thought maybe I knew it all. "The writing will be so much easier when I get to spider," I thought. You were, after all, the totem of my first book, *The Spinning Wheel*. "Spin from your own dark center," you told me when I did not know where to begin the weaving. Remember? We worked together in the attic of an old house. It felt very Cronish: you know, old woman working on the spinning wheel in the attic...

I know, you told me it was finished. You cut the thread and left. I remember that moment very clearly. In fact, I have it recorded in my journal.

September 11, 1994, "Spider Dream":

It came, it seemed, from the center of my brow—as if suddenly born. "Kill it!" my brother said. "It is dangerous." I watched the spider grow larger than any spider I had ever seen. Before my eyes it grew taller, as tall a me. Fear rose in me. "Just open the door," I said. "Let her out the door!" I saw the door was open. Then she was gone.

I awoke with a splitting headache. What was that about? I puzzled; and at the same time, knew. My first book, The Spinning Wheel, *was within one week of publication. I had to let it go. Still, I was troubled by the empty feeling the dream brought. It had not occurred to me that "something" would actually leave once the book was complete. But She was indeed gone. Call it Muse, call it totemic guidance, call it inspiration—She no longer spun from within me. Grandmother Spider had walked out the door. I felt bereft.*

You were the Muse of my first book. No doubt about that. I did want to ask you about one thing, however. This habit you have of being born from people's foreheads— is that why the Pueblo people called you "Thinking Woman," Sussistanako, because you were Thought? And in the Hopi myth, too, I remember how you focused your intent and spun out those very first threads, sent them vibrating through space to make the first connections. I can almost hear you snort. (How is it that spiders can snort like a Crone?) You always remind me what a humble housekeeper you are, hanging out in corners and so on, but I find you *everywhere* so couldn't you also have been at the beginning of time?

But get this. There are even rumors that it was *you* in the form of a beautiful maiden, who was born from the brow of Zeus. You sneaky old thing! Even if he did swallow the Mother, Metis: "Female Wisdom." I can imagine what *his* headache was like! But you fooled them. "Call me Athene," you said. And they did. They were so used to seeing you in your cronish garb, that they did not at first recognize you as Wisdom. You can't just swallow Female Wisdom, after all. It gets born again. Then they mistook your quickness at cutting threads—as love of war. I can see by your stare that you think I should mention you *do* have a fierceness. You net what you need and get the men out of your life when it's time. You end a world and then just go ahead and spin another.

The truth is, Mathilde, you have kind of a bad reputation among some folk. Are you still singing that song lyric by Paula Cole? How does it go? *"I'll just bite your head off. You call me a bitch in heat and I'll call you a Mother Fucker!"* Well—that's what I mean. People think you have a bad attitude But I think it's because you hang out with that Old Crone Hecate at The Three Way Place. It has a bad reputation you know. They say it's where choices are made and paths change. I can tell by your stare–you're thinking, "I should care?" as you go on turning the wheel, spinning, weaving, cutting. Spinning, weaving, cutting.

Around and around. Don't you ever get tired? I know, you don't want me to bring up the wife thing again. But you *are* quite a housekeeper. Patient, industrious, perseverant—the Penelope stuff. Waiting. Every night your work destroyed. Every day weaving the web anew. All those women, with names like yours, at their spinning wheels—making clothing, making food, making art, making families, making stories, making worlds. In some way, Mathilda, you remind me of my mother. She loved to make things of thread and yarn—tablecloths, bedspreads, sweaters, and shawls. One of my lasting images of her is her hands rhythmically working the needles, weaving the latest creation as it grew day by day larger in her lap. Meinrad Craighead said that once she asked her mother what she thought about when she sat in the evenings and sewed. Her mother replied, "I don't think, I am re-membering. When I am sewing, I hold you all together." My mother wouldn't have articulated this, but it is what she did: she held us all together in the countless ways she created family. But my mother was also tired. She worked hard, and much of the work because she had to. I guess you'd say, Necessity. She only cut the thread at the end, when she died, wearing the beautiful shawl she had crocheted with her hands. Sometimes, I wear that shawl and think of her and the comfort she gave.

I followed her pattern for sixteen years, and then I began to feel empty. I had lost connection to my own source. I didn't know how to fill myself up. I remember thinking I was like a "landing strip," that my children and husband came home, filled up, got repaired, and then took off again—on schedule, while I cleaned up and spent the day getting ready for the next landing. Mathilda, I know you're thinking that I'm the one with the bad attitude— that you learned that Paula Cole song from me. But there are stories that you kill your mate. I know you think it was "just time," the cycle was done. Still, you sometimes have a very nasty sting. And this thing about biting his head off— yikes! But I would agree that the thread ran out on my world at that time. I lost the connection. Yes, I did spin again, and then again. You've watched me weave and end several worlds, and weave again. Well, all right, so I did bite his head off once or twice.

But we were talking about your reputation not mine. I remember how frightened I was of you as a child. My mother frequently warned me about you: a Death Mother, who hung out in dark spaces. But I liked dark spaces, too. For instance, underneath that big cement porch in California. So like a cave. I saw you there. You wore a red hour glass on your belly. I suppose you were trying to tell me that YOU were the one who determined when time ran out. You didn't bite me, but you could have. I guess that's the point isn't it, Arachne? You always seem pleased when I remember your family name. I imagine it is irritating to be considered a bug when actually you eat bugs! Then, too, you come from a family related to the royal family of Egypt; you are really an Arachnid with a scorpion sister who is a Death Goddess like you. The one that lives in Egypt. Selket, isn't that her name? (Alright, I won't mention the ticks!)

You have to admit, Mathilda, that you do have a lot of different names and forms for one who is so specifically spider. This is why I keep asking you: what is the story I am supposed to tell? What's that you say? You don't know why I call you Mathilda? I thought you knew I named you after the Ta Ke Ti Na teacher, a beautiful woman from

Berlin with shiny blond hair. She and her partner spent two evenings in The Forest House teaching about twenty of us to use simple rhythm and sound patterns until we became a single organism, a tribe moving in synchronicity. It was shortly after this that you appeared at my hearth. I thought perhaps our sounding had brought you. But that evades the question: What is it I am supposed to write about you?

 IN YOUR MUSE:

1. In your partiuclar art form, create "The Faces of Spider Woman":

"She Who Inhabits Darkness at the Beginning of Time"

"She Who Sits at the Center and Sings"

"She Who Weaves us all Together"

"She Who Cuts the Thread"

2. In your particular art form, create an archetypal landscape called "The Three Way Place" (Crossroads—where a choice must be made)

Add images to your Spider Woman Deck.

The Spider and the Bee

T oday as I sat on the couch talking on the phone to my daughter, a spider suddenly appeared as if it had come right through the couch cover. Then it hurried across the couch and down the other side. Was that before, or after, my daughter told me her dream? Or did it happen as she spoke. "I have to tell you this dream," she said. I could hear little Sam in the background splashing in his bath. "I was talking to you on the phone, when a large bee flew in the room and stung me three times on my hand. It didn't hurt and I wasn't upset (she has a childhood fear of bees). Immediately, a small spider appeared on my hand and spun her web between the stings. She made a triangle."

I had not talked to my daughter about my spider musings, or the question I had been asking of spider. This is not the first time, however, that she and I have had powerful dream connections. Always, it is a mystery to me how archetypal images come into dream and vision, especially when you are innocent of their meaning on the conscious level. The spider, the bee, the triangle—none of these were familiar symbols to my daughter. She had no doubt, however, that the message of her dream was important, and that she needed to uncode its language. Both the spider and the bee are ancient archetypes of the goddess. Both have been totemically important to me in the last fifteen years. The spider because I, too, am a spinner of thought, of words, of stories. The spider because I had to learn, maybe a little late in life, that this spinning must come from my own center, that it has its own rhythm and its own time. The bee is another story, one that is hard for me to tell because it is so precious to me.

Once I read that what you loved as a child will return to you in later years—giving you a feeling of coming back home. Sometimes I think the forest came to me like that—because I played in creeks and forests as a child, climbed trees, made houses of ferns. Perhaps this is true, as well, of my affinity for bees. My grandfather was a bee-keeper. Honey was a natural companion crop to his fruit orchards. I remember summer on my grandfather's farm as the smell of ripe peaches and the golden hum of bees. Sometimes, we would find and capture a swarm of bees hanging from a tree like some huge overripe fruit. Other times, I would go along to watch as my grandfather, looking like a large bear, armed with smoke-gun and net mask, took frames of honey from the hives. My grandfather had a fatal heart attack while thinning peaches on his 85th birthday. For several years after his death, I would dream of him on his birthday, working with his peaches, surrounded by a golden hum. Always my memories of him are filled with sunshine, the hum of bees, ripe fruit, golden honey. It was on this shaft of memory that the bee came into my life one sunny day many years later—and forever changed me.

It was unusually warm for a February Day, and beautiful in the garden where eight of us had gathered. We lay on the deck in the sunshine and were gently led on a journey down the river Nile to meet the Goddess Isis. I cannot speak of the other journeyers or even the details of the journey, for I sailed so easily into goddess—and was gone. I do remember it was Valentine's Day, when I journeyed down the river and my heart burst open. I don't know how long I was there. I know I didn't want to leave. "Remember you can come back any time," She said to me.

Those around me were urging me up. Everyone, it seemed, was already back in the circle talking. On the deck, sitting in the golden sun, I heard someone say, "There's a big bee in the sky," Later, I discovered he had said, "There's a big V (of geese)." In the moment, I heard the hum. "My grandfather was a bee keeper," I said to the man sitting next to me, as the hum grew large. I waited for it to pass by me. But no. The vibration came, instead, directly into my solar plexus. I was vibrating, expanding, rushing, seeing my own fuzzy gold and black, bee striped belly, buzzing through the trees, garden below...

I panicked—and cried out for grounding. A friend grounded my feet, and I came back into my body. But the hum was still large within me. *I* was not humming—it was humming me. Then the hum surrounded us and the eight of us were vibrating like a hive of bees. Gold light was all around us. To me, it was as tangible as pollen, gold dust falling. In that moment, I felt such bliss. Always remember this, I told myself, even then knowing I would forget and re-member, forget and re-member.

For days, the vibration was very strong; I could not keep myself from humming, which was sometimes a problem since I was teaching English in a community college. Even more of a problem was that I was not the same. Within a year, my personal relationship had ended, as well as several friendships. I do not mean to imply that this was an easy time. My heart was torn and I went through a long period of grieving. But I could not turn back. The structures I had spent years building no longer worked for me. And I knew, as well, that this did not just *happen* to me—I had asked. I had asked how I could serve the goddess, how I could serve the earth. Now I needed the courage to do the work I had been given.

Within three years, I had resigned as a full time teacher in Academia, moved from a 2,000 square foot suburban home into an 8x10 hand-built shed in the forest, and begun the project that was to become Wanderland. Up until that February day twelve years ago, I was not a person who sang, hummed, or sounded. Now I could hear the singing, not only in myself but around me and in the earth. Although the vibration that the bee brought into me has since been tempered by time and experience, you could say that from that moment, I have never been totally silent. Sound became part of me. I use it to send prayer and to sing to the earth; I travel on it when I journey; I use it in healing to move energy and light.

I have never been able to "explain" the bee experience, even to myself. It was not a journey of imagination, a dream, or even a journey into the shamanic "other world." What I experienced was physically real in the moment. I am not sure what would have happened if I had let go and not cried out for grounding. Would I have returned to my body? Reading the Hopi Creation tale, I am reminded of this experience. For me, it was the time of the "yellow light," when "breath" and vibration came into me, and when my heart opened to the "creator."

Bee goddess on a Boeotian amphora 700 BC

Curiously, I didn't have a clue at the time that bees were associated with the Goddess, that this imagery went back at least as far as Neolithic times. It did not take me long to discover, however, that the bee has an ancient mythological history. The Minoans were bee keepers and passed that knowledge on to the Greeks. Images of the "Bee Lady" and "Bee Priestesses" appear in the art of both cultures. The Goddesses Demeter, Aphrodite, and Artemis were all associated with the bee, and their priestesses were called "Melissa"—bee. In a stunning scene from the novel, *The Fifth Sacred Thing,* Starhawk brings back the magic of these ancient priestesses when her central character, Madrone, receives an initiation from the Melissa: *"Don't fight the change." She heard the Melissa's voice, coming to her not in words but in a rasping vibration, a tone in the air, a scent. "Let go. Let go." She was falling; then she was flying. Lilac was not a name but a realm of the air that called her into places where her whole body throbbed with delight. Sage was a universe, pungent, bracing. Hold on! her human mind cried. "Let go," the Melissa buzzed and hummed and murmured.*[5] Reading this scene, some seven years after my own experience, brought me close to tears. "It *is* real," I thought, and "I simply stumbled into it in the innocence of my open heart and desire." Still, the vehicle, the pathway for my experience seems to have come from a deep memory of the bee's vibration. Would it have come if I had not had this memory? I do not know.

I do know, however, that bees are remarkable insects. Actually, they are just plain remarkable—insect or not. You don't have to read very far into their habits and social organization to understand why they would hold such significance in early cultures. They are the only insects, for instance, capable of maintaining themselves continuously as a colony through successive generations. And they do this with a storehouse of food that they gather and make from the gold dust of pollen. This ability to make honey, a powerful life-food and preservative, is at least partly why the bee, along with the butterfly, is associated symbolically with regeneration.

Bees communicate with each other in a language of circles and spirals which they create in intricate patterns of dance that signal other bees the distance and direction of a food source. They align these patterns with the sun to indicate direction like a compass. In a similar way, their social organization is clearly imprinted with purpose. It is matriarchal with the queen as its center—and also incredibly pragmatic. You are born knowing exactly what your role is—no fussing and fretting about your purpose in life. You are also born with the gifts needed to fulfill that purpose. The hind legs of the workers, for instance, are made with both pollen scrapers and pollen baskets.

The majority of the hive are sterile female workers, whose tasks are to give undivided attention to taking care of the hive and feeding the young. In fact, they even know exactly how much time is allotted for each job: the first three days they spend cleaning the cells of the hive and feeding on pollen honey mixtures; the next five days, they feed larvae with salivary secretions and bee bread; for six days they build new cells from wax secreted from their wax glands; for three days they convert nectar into honey by fanning; then they spend a day patrolling in front of the hive. On the 21st day, they start gathering nectar and pollen until they die a few days later. The life span of the female workers is, then, remarkably close to the moon's cycle—and they wear the moon crescents as their antennae, a detail emphasized in the ancient images. In their role of service to the hive and to the queen, they are reminiscent of the priestess of ancient goddess cultures.

The male or "drone's" sole purpose is to fertilize the egg. The act of doing so instantly kills him. There is only one queen bee to a hive. It is she who gives purpose to all activity. Not only this, but she is the result of a "virgin" birth. That is, she is born from an unfertilized egg which has been fed high protein, royal jelly produced from the salivary glands of the workers. The queen, the center of the hive and the source of creation, lays all the eggs. She is a remarkable natural archetype for the goddess, the creatrix.

In her initiation, Starhawk's character, Madrone, merges with each aspect of bee. She is drone: *"spiraling higher and higher in the air, quickened to life for the one mad moment of flight that was life's purpose, wings whipping the air in pursuit of the golden flying body that was the aim of all desire."* She is worker: *"moving in the dark safe hive, where body brushed against scented body, learning from movement and smell what the hive knew, the paths through the air to the nectar flow, the health of the brood, the golden warmth of the sun."* She is queen: *" emerging with strong wings out of the womb-dark hive to soar for the first and only time up into the light, up and up, her strong wings beating the sweet air, chased by a cloud of drones. Only the strongest could catch her, could plunge himself into her in one ecstatic midair moment and fill her with the brood to come."*[6] It is hard for Madrone to come back into the "clumsiness" of the human body, but when she finally does, her senses are so highly tuned that language seems inadequate compared to the subtleties of taste and smell she experienced as bee. When she does come back, she has within her the vibration—and the instinct of knowing the right path.

The gift the bee gives is knowing how to "become" what Spider Woman teaches in *The Book of the Hopi.* The bee people, in fact, are quite similar to the "first people" in the Hopi Creation story: both understand who they are and their purpose; both are instinctively connected to the "Creator" through vibration and sound. Language is added almost as an afterthought. Spider Mother calls out to Sotuknang to return and give the people speech so they can talk to each other. It is the tricky gift of speech, however, that leads to the destruction of the First World. The Talker appears in the form of a bird, Mochni (like a mocking bird). He cannot stop talking, and the more he talks, the more he convinces them of the differences between the people and the animals, and the differences between the people themselves because of the color of their skins, their speech, and their beliefs in the plan of the Creator. This is when separation occurs: the animals draw away from the people and the people draw away from each other and from the Creator.

In *The Book of the Hopi* Spider is the Mother of Wisdom. She wraps each newly created being in her Wisdom cape; she sings to them the songs of Wisdom and of Love. She is spinner, weaver, cutter. She is the triune wheel that turns the cycles of life. This can be visualized symbolically by drawing a triangle, placing a dot at its center, and drawing the spokes to the three corners. Thus the yoni of the goddess contains the wheel of change. On my wall is a large print of Meinrad Craighead's painting "Wisdom." Inside the white egg of creation, which is born out of surrounding darkness, Craighead has painted the triune wheel, and within it the three stages of the moon–crescent born of the darkness, full, and waning, back to the darkness, and always—the underlying womb of darkness from which life comes. Looking at this image, I am reminded, as people for millennium have been reminded by the moon, that the three—the triangle—has within it continual change and renewal. This is, of course, why it is also the symbol of the Triune Goddess.

I am also reminded of a passage from *The Book of the Hopi*: "Some of the people retained the wisdom granted them upon their Emergence. With this wisdom they understood that the farther they proceeded on the Road of Life and the more they developed, the harder it was. That was why their world was destroyed every so often to give them a fresh start." [7] As I look back through the twelve years of growing since the bee flew into my life, I know that it not only clarified my life purpose but also kicked me into action, even though there are times that I moan and complain—it *is* work, after all— and even though I do not know when I will be asked to let go again in order to move closer still to the center place.

 IN YOUR MUSE:

1. Listen for **The Talker** in your own conversations and in those around you. (He can't stop talking. You will hear him creating separation by emphasizing the differences between people and between people and the earth.) After a day or so of this awareness, journal his monologues or create his portrait.

2. **Beeing:** Observe yourself for a week—journaling at the end of each day the moments you felt most alive, most content, most purposeful.

3. Create a landscape or a collage of what you loved as a child.

4. **Triune:** Create a Mandalic design with the archetype of the Triune Wheel (The Wheel of Change). Start by drawing a circle (symbolizing the Cauldron of Creation).

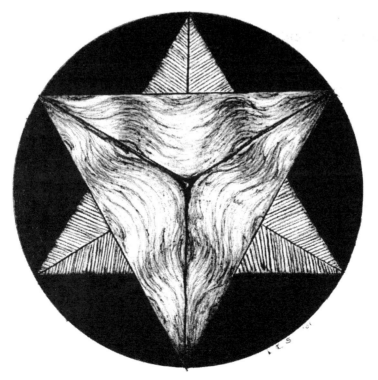

Triune Wheel of Creation

Place a dot in the center of the circle (symbolizing the place of continual renewal). Within the circle, draw an equilateral triangle that touches the edges of the circle. From the center place, draw lines to the corners of the triangle (symbolizing the Wheel of Change).

Notice that you can again create the triune wheel within each of the three triangles by placing the dot in the center and drawing the spokes. And then you can do this again with the smaller triangles, and then again and again. Infinitely. This gives you a sense of why three and nine are Triune Goddess numbers, and why this design is a symbol of the many faces of the Triune Goddess, symbolized within the names Crone, Maiden, Mother.

At any point in the evolution of your design, begin to paint or collage the design to symbolize the constantly turning wheel of life that arises from the Cauldron of Creation—maiden, mother, crone; waxing, full, waning; spring, summer, fall; bud, flower, fruit...(Add images of your changing self in this design)

(For another approach to the Wheel of Change see The Spinning Wheel, *pp. 114-118.)*

Add images to your Spider Woman Deck.

Over the Edge

Today, I went over the edge of the County Line. A front page feature article about my work was censored by a widely distributed county newspaper, The County Line. The event has given me pause for reflection although I can't say that I was totally surprised when the call came from the frustrated reporter. "The editor says he can't print anything about mythology," she said. "It might offend their readers." My first response was actually relief. I wanted to fly helium balloons in purple, gold, and red, over my mailbox I felt so liberated.

For a month I had lived in fear of Friday's mail—to reach into that green box and pull out my own face on the front page of the County Line, not knowing, of course, what-the-hell image they might have chosen—me fondling a mushroom, me posing with a five foot cedar bear, me waving my finger in passionate speech for the forest, or just me looking haggish, mouth ajar, staring back. I even had a few exposure nightmares—one where I walked into the presence of my father wearing see-through clothes.

Just the week before, the reporter had called me, stunned by the news that the paper wanted her to remove all references to Joseph Campbell from the article because of "reader response." "Joseph Campbell?" I replied, equally stunned. "I thought Joseph Campbell was a household word." I wandered around in the forest for awhile that day, wondering—"where do I live, anyway, that Joseph Campbell cannot be mentioned in a county newspaper? If Joseph Campbell is banned, what about me?"

Today I got the answer. I, too, have gone over the county line. A part of me is pleased by this. After all I join the company of Joseph Campbell. And like Joseph, I , too, think of myself as somewhat of a maverick. I've always resisted lines. However, the experience does remind me, with a jolt, that I am not always "at home" in the place where I live. And my mind begins bouncing through memory like a random ball hitting upon this time and that when, indeed, I felt "out of place."

Last night in the community meeting on forest management—"We cannot afford to let our *inventory* just sit there for a hundred years," the timber industry spokesman said. "Besides if we let the trees get that old, you can be sure the environmentalists would start demonstrating in the streets to save them." My stomach knots. I look at the people around me and become self conscious of the way I am dressed—my purple tie dye and black velvet jacket. Hopelessness floods through me. How do I begin to explain that the forest is so much more.

Two weeks ago our county held a "Futures Forum," where the public was asked to brainstorm ideas for managing *our* natural *resources* for future generations." Is there anywhere to mention the value of wilderness—apart from us?" I finally ask, after two hours of listening. "Wilderness *is* natural resources," was the reply. "No. It is not," I said, feeling as if I spoke a foreign language, feeling as if I were from another time, or maybe just another planet.

My family reunion, scheduled for the summer, begins to loom large in my mind—a brother who sees spirit as emotional nonsense; a brother who is a timber industry executive; a brother who sees mythology as "Satanism;" an uncle who refers to environmentalists as "tree huggers" and even "stump huggers," who rails against environmental emotionalism; an uncle whose house is filled with stuffed trophies from hunting adventures. One thing is true about them all—they are passionate, as am I, about what they see and who they are. But if I am an alien even in my own family, where am I at home?

Truth is, it has always been fairly easy for me to feel like an outsider. I love the little myth Clarissa Pinkola Estes creates to lend distance and humor to the discomfort of that experience. "Your family thinks you're an alien. You have feathers, they have scales. Your idea of a good time is the forest, the wilds, the inner life, the outer majesty. Their idea of a good time is folding towels. If this is so for you in your family, then you are a victim of the Mistaken Zygote Syndrome... The Zygote Fairy was flying over your hometown one night, and all the little zygotes in her basket were hopping and jumping with excitement... You were indeed destined for parents who would have understood you, but, oops, you fell out of the basket over the wrong house... Your real family was three miles farther on." [8] But Clarissa—the wrong county? Maybe even the wrong time?

Spider Mother, you who know the secret of circles and of webs; Spider Mother, you who weave us all together, let me feel my belonging. Let me be in-home.

We come from many directions up and down the valley, to form a circle on the beach on the eve of the Spring Equinox. The wind sweeps clouds fast across the sky and for a moment there is a glow on the horizon before the sun is gone, and the wind softens. I look around the circle, twenty some people of all ages bundled against the cold. They look strangely unfamiliar in the dusky light. I am wishing I were warmer, when the bundled shape next to me turns into my friend, Kathleen, who pulls an extra pair of gloves from her cloak and hands them to me with a hug.

Then the chant begins and our voices blend with the ocean and the wind: *Take the gift of love and death. Take the gift of blood and bone. Weave a circle breath by breath. Build a vision stone by stone.* Over and over the chant sweeps through us and then stops. In the silence we ask "What is our vision in this time of new growth?" Then we speak, one by one, around the circle. Some speak of balance, some speak of abundance, some speak of personal challenge. Each spins a thread of desire to the center; each is different—and the same. The chant begins again: *Take the gift of love and death. Take the gift of blood and bone. Weave a circle breath by breath. Build a vision stone by stone.*

Still chanting, we begin the journey, one at a time, through the pathways of the labyrinth, clearly outlined in the sand. Chanting, walking, step by step we make our individual journey to the center. At the center where the powers meet, where the tree of life grows, we each offer our vision, send our prayer. Then we return, step by step, along the labyrinthine spiral until we emerge from the pathway and form a circle again, arms around each other, chanting and swaying as one. *Weave a circle breath by breath. Build a vision stone by stone.*

I look around the circle at these friends, their faces lit by moonlight. For a moment, our voices seem to deepen and in the overtone, I hear Spider Mother's clear, sweet song, as she weaves us all together, wrapping us in her silver white cloak. I am in-home.

Later I drive slowly along the moonlit ocean, then follow the Nehalem River valley toward home. Surely I live in paradise, I think to myself. On a full moon night such as this, pastures become luminous ponds of light, mountains black shapes against the sky. For a short distance, the road follows close enough to the river to see it, too, silvered by the moon. Once this river was filled with living silver, great runs of salmon making their way back to the place of their birth. The Native People called them "Ancestors," for they so clearly carried the memory of the way back home. We now think that it is smell that guides them, smell that flows through their body, their body so like water, fluidly silver. Knowing—they swim back to the source, the place where their creative center explodes in masses of eggs. And then they die, offering their bodies to the living stream and to future generations. River god/dess flowing, letting go.

I turn left, away from the mainstem of the river, and follow Coal Creek into the foothills toward the forest where I live. The road ends and I follow a narrow country lane to the driveway of Wanderland. I am still enamored of coming around the bend in the driveway and seeing The Forest House lit up against the dark of the forest. Each time, I see it newly, surprised that it is there. Eleven years of work telescope into just this moment: the tents, the shed, the mud, the cold, the rodents, the hard physical work—and before any of that, a dream. All are part of a story I tell—become somehow "past." Even stranger that people now come to The Forest House, seeing it as if it were always there.

Still, for me, it is not really *about* building a house. It is about an eleven year relationship with this place. I know the dirt, the stones, the plants. I know the smell of the air in different seasons and the changing voice of the creek. I know each board of the house, each shingle, even the trenches of the foundation I know, inch by inch. Every where I look there are stories to tell. Here where I park my car were two old trailers, so overgrown by twenty years of abandonment, that we had to search for them in what seemed a dense, endless, wilderness. They became two tons of garbage we hauled on tarps down the hill and loaded into a huge U-Haul truck, but that was only after clearing the driveway up to this spot, and that was only after discovering that there was the imprint of an old logging road to follow underneath the thickets and ferns and trees, and before that even was the exploring.

And still, I have not told you the stories but have only shown you where a few of them are. By now, there have become so many, it is impossible to tell them all—and not necessary. Simply the fact that they are there—a varied tapestry, a rich web of connections—grounds me in this place. Ocean, valley, river, forest, this house, the work of my hands through the turning of the seasons—all are intricately woven. Somehow, I have found my way back home. This is my "House of Belonging."*

IN YOUR MUSE:

1. What place comes to mind when you think of "home"? What stories connect you to this place? Give them titles.

2. In your particular art form, create an Archetypal Landscape: "House of Belonging."

*In his poem, "House of Belonging," David Whyte says:

> *"This is the bright home*
> *in which I live,*
> *this is where*
> *I ask*
> *my friends*
> *to come,*
> *this is where I want*
> *to love all the things*
> *it has taken me so long to learn to love."*

Add images to your Spider Woman Deck.

You <u>Can</u> Go Home Again

L ooking back through the years, I see the many worlds I have spun and let go. Some I severed in pain and grief. Others, like spider webs in the wind, simply collapsed, much as I desired them to stay. I remember the early spring day, after my father's memorial service, when I drove away from my childhood home for the last time. For over forty years, I had been coming back to that small, two bedroom bungalow where my parents lived, where I had been a teenager, and where I was always welcomed "home." There, I was special for no reason except that I was a child of that home and remembered from the beginning of my life, in stories, in pictures, in love. Within a month after my father's death, the pictures had been sorted, the recesses of the attic and shop emptied of years and years of family history, the house stripped and sold.

On that March day, when I drove down the freeway through the Willamette River valley, away from my childhood home, I knew I could never return except in memory and in dream. My reality felt like a handful of sand pouring through my fingers. I realized the rain had stopped only when my windshield wipers began to make scraping noises on the dry glass. Then I saw that in the break between showers the light had turned gold. Fields of new grass glowed iridescently green. Then the cars around me began to pull over to the side of the highway and stop. "What's happening?" I thought, at the same moment that I saw three perfect rainbows, one after another, arched across the glowing grass into the blue of heaven. There was nothing to do but stop. People were taking pictures. I simply stood. "Thank you," I said, knowing that always I would remember this, the time of the three rainbows, as the moment when my childhood home went back to Dreamtime.

Knowing it is there, in that place of rich abundance, in vivid images and memories, always part of who I am, always part of the new worlds I weave, nurtures me still and connects me to a source deeper even than place or house. Here, too, I find the richness of my grandfather's farm, memories of the home I created for my own children and their growing, and the deep loves that have shaped me and given richness to my life. Perhaps it is a sign of Cronedom, that sometimes I sit and simply watch memories shift and change, like spider webs that catch, for a moment, rainbow light as they shimmer across the void and vanish. Memory comes through all of the senses. Sometimes a smell, a sound, or a certain cast of light will take me with sudden emotion to a moment in the past, and I feel the flash of that world and what it was like to be the person I was in that place and time. And then I let go, watching as it vanishes into the deep well of creating, a part of the new worlds I weave.

"The spider's web shows the possibility of unifying space from a divine center," as

James Cowan points out.[9] It does not, however, illustrate that what we are connected to will always remain the same. We are "orphaned" by severing our connection to the center, not by change. When Sea Otter Woman tells Ice in the Nehalem story, "You will not find your way home again," she simply names his spiritual affliction; for driven by impatience and hunger, he breaks the thread of connection. The curse of Ice—and frequently the curse of humanity, as well—is to feel orphaned, lost, a wanderer in search of home. Many cultures have not only a myth (a memory) of a garden where we were once at home with all beings, but also the story of separation from that place of harmony. Perhaps it is human destiny to make this journey of separation in order to develop, and balance, powers of the mind and will that are the unique gifts of being human. It does seem, however, that the lessons of that particular initiation are becoming more and more evident, and that the challenge has changed to how can we feel connected again, how can we find our way back home?

Science uses a metaphor drawn from spider teachings to show us that "home" is a web of relationships, many we are only just beginning to understand, and that nothing can be viewed separately for it is the interconnections that make the living whole. This they call "ecology." The root "ec" means home. The net of Indra in Hindu mythology is a similar metaphor. In the heavenly abode of the great god Indra there hangs a spectacular net stretched out in all directions into infinity. A sparkling jewel, a dew drop, rests in each eye of the net. Since the net is infinite, the jewels are also infinite. If you look closely at a single jewel, you will see reflected in its polished surfaces all the other jewels in the net, infinite in number. As you look deeper, you will see that each of the jewels reflected in this one jewel is also reflecting all the other jewels, so that the reflections are infinite. When any part of the web is touched, the whole intricate network vibrates and reflects the change.

The Navajo use this broader understanding of "home" as a web of connections in their healing ritual, *The Beauty Way*. To be in dis-ease is to be out of harmony within one's house. This "house" is not only body, but relationship to each other and to the living earth:

> *In Tsegihi (oh you who dwell!)*
> *In the house made of dawn,*
> *In the house made of evening twilight,*
> *In the house made of the dark cloud,*
> *In the house made of the he-rain,*
> *In the house made of the dark mist,*
> *In the house made of the she-rain,*
> *In the house made of pollen,*
> *In the house made of grasshoppers,*

Where the dark mist curtains the doorway,
The path to which is on the rainbow
from the Navajo, "House Made of Dawn"

In this powerful ritual, performed by the person's community and lasting many days, the one in dis-ease lies in the center of a healing circle that has been drawn on the earth, using symbols and color that evoke their relationship to earth/spirit/community/family/body/self. The gifts of Spider Woman—vibration, color, and sound—are used within this ritual in the continuous chanting and prayer, which plays on the correspondence between the vibration of a color and of a sound tuned to the vibration of the chakras. In turn, the chakras are tuned to the vibratory pole of the earth. Hence, healing is brought about by bringing the person back into "attunement" with the whole web. [10]

The symbol of the spider's web, the circle of connections evolving from the center, shows not only the possibility of unifying space from the center, but also the ability to go back to that center. In the creation story of the Hopi, Spider Woman teaches the people that this can be done through our love of the Creator and the creation expressed in song, chant, and prayer. In Australian Aboriginal cultures this teaching is made concrete by the shamanic ability to "solidify" the air and travel on a thread between worlds. James Cowan describes how the Australian Aboriginal "Karadji" (Shaman) demonstrates this reality to the people: The Karadji would *arrive along a pathway from the west, leaving the main body of the tribe at the corroboree ground. Here a bull roarer, the voice of Baiame, would be sounded prior to a period of singing. The singing induced a meditative or trance-like state conducive to magical performance. Lying on their backs under a tree, the clever-men would sing out their buruimaulwe, or testes cord, which in turn evolved into their respective maulwe, secreting gossamer. They would then begin climbing up the cord, hand over hand, until they reached the top of the tree. When the bull roarer sounded again, these men would descend the tree.* [11]

This account is a living metaphor of our ability to ascend and descend the tree of life, which is at our own center. This understanding is part of our ancient wisdom heritage that comes to us from many different cultures—Native American, European, Asian, African. It is often symbolized by the snake that lives at the base of the tree of life, that awakens and sleeps, ascends and descends. This is the energy (Kundalini) that climbs our spine, our own tree of life. This is the vibratory energy, opening through the chakras, that Spider Mother tunes to the central pole of the earth. A lifetime may be spent in opening the potential of this gift. It is also cultivated by continually practicing the simple act of "grounding," breathing our energy down through our root into the earth and back up through our body and out our crown. *(see p. 12)* For our own root chakra is our connection to the earth and corresponds to the vibration of the earth. In grounding, we also connect ourselves to the vitality of our past and the potential of our future—and we realign ourselves with earth and spirit.

The Karadji dramatically demonstrate that humans have "web spinning" abilities; that they can "solidify the air" by focusing their intention. In singing out their sexual energy as a cord, an "aerial ladder," The Karadji show not only the connection between spiritual and physical but also the power of human will to shape energy. In this way, thought and dreaming create the initial patterns that become form. This is perhaps the most important message of the complexly beautiful Hopi Creation Story. Spider Woman teaches that we, too, are creators—that what we focus on, what we imagine, what we give our energy to, becomes the reality around us.

Lately, I have been drawn to standing in the center, pulled as if by instinct, or perhaps by a hunger, reeling me back home. Last week I wandered through a gnarly little pine forest, a fragment surrounded by developments along one of my favorite beaches. The ground under the trees was still brown from winter and the darkness of the canopy above. To my surprise, a perfect moss circle, about five feet in diameter, glowed before me in a brilliant chartreus green. How could I resist taking the few steps to its center, and singing out my song to the little forest around me, sending my roots deep into the earth, letting go into the deep well of my own creation. As I relaxed down into myself and felt the energy flow back up my body, the forest glowed around me and I was a part of it. Then, as I looked around, I realized that there was not just one, but many glowing moss circles within this little forest, each with a center that seemed to call out its magical potential. And I knew that no matter where I stood, I would be in the center.

 IN YOUR MUSE:
Creating Spider Woman Mandalas

In Sanskrit *mandala* literally means circle and center. Its traditional design often uses the circle—symbol of the cosmos, and the square—symbol of the earth and of human creation. The center is symbolic of eternal potential. From this "inexhaustible source all seeds grow and develop, all cells realize their function; even down to the atom there is none without its nucleus, its sun-seed about which revolve its component particles. As in the atom, so in the stars..." (Jose Arguelles, *Mandala*, 1984)

Carl Jung found that people instinctively draw circles and mandalic patterns in doodling, and seem to find it comforting. He called mandalas "mirrors of the soul," and found them useful for meditation and healing because they remind us that we unify our world from the center (the source). This is the teaching of Spider Mother as well. She weaves the design into creation.

1. Web of Connection: At the center of a circle, place a symbol that represents your growing self. Within the circle, collage, paint, or draw symbols for what is most important to you. (Each of these can become a mandalic pattern as well, radiating out other meanings like the jewels in Indra's web.) Let placement, size, and detail of these images reflect how you are related to them (i.e. close, far, part of, in thought, in dreamtime.) Draw or paint threads of connection. Let the threads reflect the tone, emotion, and strength of the connections.

2. Mandala of Becoming: *"She sits in the center, where the tree of life grows and sings to the mystery that flows from the four."*

To create this Spider Mother Mandala follow these steps:

Step one: Record or have someone read the following guided meditation to you. Be sure you are in a comfortable and uninterrupted space.

Breathe, release tension, and ground. Allow your roots to go deeply into the earth. See yourself sitting on the earth in a place that is special to you. You sit at the center of a circle. Breathe and feel yourself at the center.

As you sit here in the center, be aware of the larger circle around you: the light from the rising sun in the East illuminates and flows through you. You breathe the inspiration of a new dawning. The sun warms your body as morning gives way to mid-day and spring to summer in the fires of the South. Feel the warmth growing inside you, leaping in the fires of creativity.

As the sun begins to cool into evening, like summer into fall, the mists and rains begin to fall around you. You see the moon appear in the darkening sky, pulling the tides of the oceans, pulling the waters within you. You open to this birthing flow, letting go to the night, letting go to the turning of winter in the North. In your body, in your hands, in your voice, you begin to feel the stirring, the life impulse rising to take form, to take shape.

Breathe. Fill yourself with the awareness of being at the center of this circle. As you inhale, feel the powers flowing to the center from the four directions, filling you with the gifts of your creativity. As you exhale, feel the spinning out from the center, the spinning out of your creations.

What are you spinning out in your life right now? What are the main threads you are creating? Notice what they look like. Visualize them spinning out from the center. What color are they? How strong? What is their texture? How much impulse propels them? How do they move? (as spokes, spirals, circles, waves?)

Continue to breathe in, feeling the inflow of the circle to the center; and to breathe out, watching the outflow of creation. When you are ready, breathe yourself back to present time.

Step two: Draw the circle. Put at the center a symbol for your essential self or your creative source.

Step three: Draw, color, or symbolize the four powers as you experienced them.

Step four: Draw, color, or symbolize the outflow of creations from the center. Let these threads of creation look and move in the way you saw them in your imagining.

Step five: What colors draw forth and nurture the highest potential of these creations? Let the colors take shape or image.

Step six: What animals, plants, birds draw forth the strength of these creations?

3. Mandala of 8: The number eight is associated with Spider Mother both in the number of her legs and in the shape of her body. The number eight is about balance, the polarities joined with equal weight. In the traditional Tarot, eight is called Justice, and the image is the scales, the two sides "weighing " against each other balanced by a central pole. Archetypally, the eight, especially the eight on its side without an upper or lower position, shows the equality of polarities: of solar and lunar, of masculine and feminine. Eight on its side is also the double spiral, the sign of Infinity, of cyclic change.

In many traditions, eight holy days are celebrated in the turning of the seasonal year. Four of these are called Solar Holy Days and fall at the quarters: Spring and Fall Equinox, and Summer and Winter Solstice. Four are called Lunar Holy Days and fall at the cross-quarters: Imbolc, Beltane, Lamas, and Samhain. Artist Sheila Braun has shown the cyclic movement of these polarities in a mandalic design of the Wheel of the Year which correlates the outer cycles with our inner cycles of change.

(see The Spinning Wheel, *p. 107)*

The Eight Poles (*Note: dates may vary by one or two days.)*
    December 22, Winter Solstice, North, "She turns."
    February 2, Imbolc, Northeast, "She is reborn."
    March 21, Spring Equinox, East, "She grows."
    May 2, Beltane, Southeast, "She loves."
    June 22, Summer Solstice, South, "She shines."
    August 2, Lamas, Southwest, "She labors."
    September 22, Autumn Equinox, West, "She knows."
    October 31, Samhain, Northwest, "She dies."

 MAKING RITE:
Playing the Wheel of Eight

This ritual evolved from ritual play with Sheila Braun's mandala symbolizing the inner and outer Wheel of Change.

First lay out the mandalic line, using four pieces of heavy string or rope about six to eight feet long. Create the mandala on the directional axis: Winter Solstice in the North; Summer Solstice in the South; Spring Equinox in the East; Fall Equinox in the West. Use a spiral design or a crystal or shell to mark the center.

Next lay out the intersecting cross-quarters: Imbolc, Beltane, Lamas, and Samhain.

Write out the meaning of all eight poles on slips of paper: For example, Imbolc, *She is reborn.*

There are eight positions; however, two people can hold one pole, or one person can hold two adjacent poles, if the circle is smaller or larger than eight.

First Movement: Tell people to find their place in the circle by following impulse (rather than calling attention to the meaning of the poles).

Breathe and ground as a circle. Pick up the end of the string in front of you and the slip of paper with the pole's meaning.

Starting with where you are in seasonal cycle (Winter Solstice, Beltane...) begin the chant. Each person says the meaning of the pole they hold. Go around and around the circle, listening to the turning of the wheel. Allow the chant to become well established.

Second Movement: At the end of a complete cycle, the circle moves clockwise, and each person assumes a new pole. Let each person experience the full movement (eight poles) of integrated solar/lunar turning.

Third Movement: Play the polarities. Again starting with where you are seasonally, one person speaks the polarity and is answered by the person at the opposite pole (at the other end of the string). Do this several times; then reverse order. For example, "She turns" (Winter Solstice); "She shines (Summer Solstice). Reversed: "She shines; "She turns." Reversal helps you to let go of positive/negative and linear sequence and allows you a deeper sense of the polar dynamic.

End the ritual with journaling and passing the talking stick.

(See The Spinning Wheel, *pp. 112-120 for additional mandala exercises.*)

Add images to your Spider Woman Deck.

Family Connections

Spider teaches about family connections, and about what happens when those connections are broken. This is both an ecological and a personal message. A Nehalem Indian story tells how South Wind fell in love with Ocean's daughter and learned that he was part of the family—even though he was, indeed, quite different—as different as air is from water. And just as related.

People who live on the North Coast will tell you that South Wind loves to travel up the coast in the winter time, changing things as he goes. In the old days, he had many headbands. Sometimes he would put on his headband for making the trees dance, and just have fun as the tops swayed and swirled. When he wore this headband, he would comb Ocean's hair and white spray would fly from deep glistening waves. Sometimes he would wear the headband that broke off branches and even the tops of the trees, tossing them onto the earth and into the waters. He loved to watch Ocean dance when he wore this headband. Other times, but not as often, he would put on the most powerful of his headbands and when he walked the earth, large trees would fall. The earth shook with the sound. The forests roared like a huge beast or a giant freight train overhead. When he wore this headband, Ocean swelled with anger and tossed water and wood upon the shore.

As South Wind passed through Nehalem land, he often saw a beautiful maiden playing on the shore near the ocean. He thought of her as "Shore." Her hair was like the ocean waves, combed back, and sunlight sparkled on her skin. She was Ocean's daughter. South Wind fell in love. But every time he tried to reach her, she disappeared into the mist. One day when he saw her he looked straight into her eyes and did not look away. He took her hand and she went home with him to the Southern land. And so in love was he that sometimes South Wind forgot to visit Ocean.

But Ocean's daughter was unhappy, for the beds in the Southern Land were hard and she was homesick for the soft mists and the billowy comforts of her water-bed. Shore's skin began to dry and her hair and eyes grew dull.

Finally, South Wind took her back home to visit Ocean. Ocean and South Wind talked it over and made a deal, for they both loved Ocean's daughter and they knew that they would always be joined as a family. Since South Wind would be visiting often, he agreed to bring large wood for Ocean to chew up in the winter time when he was hungriest. South Wind knew he could bring abundant wood for it was what he did best.

And so it was. In the time when the forests grew strong and deep on the shore, South Wind walked through the trees—bending and breaking and casting them into the rivers and the sea. In this way, the life of the ocean and the rivers was fed—and the salmon swam in great abundance from river to ocean and back again. And if you looked closely, you could see Ocean's daughter playing on the shore, sparkling and changing in the dance of wind and sea. (Retold from *Nehalem Tillamook Tales*, Clara Pearson)

The Nehalem story illustrates an essential ecological connection between wind, forest, and water—a connection that feeds life. Ironically, now that we have not only clear cut many of the forests near streams and rivers but also removed large wood from the streams, we are beginning to realize that we have deprived the waters of necessary nutrients. "Our streams lack large woody debris that provide shelter, pools, and nutrients for fish," watershed assessments tell us over and over. And we work to recover the natural connection. We plant trees along the rivers. We throw frozen fish back into the streams. We hope that someday the salmon will return.

I like to think that maybe we are learning the lessons the Tricksters teach us about human will, appetite, and unconsciousness; that maybe we live in a time of "re-membering" connections and recognizing the delusion of separation. Certainly, the popularity of "eco" terms seems to indicate this: "eco-feminism," "eco-psychology," "eco-forestry," "eco-mythology." Still it is a slow process. One that continually catches me in the midst of old conditioning—usually (much to my chagrin) *just* when I think I've got it. (Sometimes, I think that I, alone, keep the Trickster very busy!) And so it happened that a few days ago, I ran into a friend while shopping. She had just been to a family get together in Ohio. It was a perfect chance for me to tell someone, again, my fears about my own family reunion coming up—and, of course, how I didn't fit in. My voice sounded loud to myself in the small store as I recited the descriptions of my family: "One brother is an executive in the timber industry; one brother thinks mythology is Satanism; one brother thinks spirit is emotional nonsense; one Uncle calls environmentalists...blah, blah, blah..." Leaving the store, I felt uncomfortable. Something was wrong.

For several days I could hear my voice reciting the descriptions—my family labeled and one-dimensional like cardboard cut-outs. Then it began to be not my voice but *a* voice that spoke over and over, focusing on the difference, focusing on the separation. Finally I realized, with some humiliation, that I had been caught. I was within the grips of "The Talker" who, the Hopi Creation Story tells us, talks and talks like a Mocking Bird, repeating over and over stories of difference, stories of separation. At that point, I decided that one of the hardest things about writing a book on mythology was that it continually asked me to change.

Because people were separated by their differences, angry and fearful of each other—Spider Woman destroyed the First World. And so I go back to re-creating. I am practicing re-membering. I re-member how my brother came unexpectedly to my son's wedding. In a downpour of rain, I came upon him suddenly in the parking lot, thinking at first he was just someone who looked like the brother I had not seen for several years. Then he smiled and called my name. My heart burst open, remembering how much I loved him. And we forgot the difference.

I remember how my uncle took me with him fishing on a summer evening when I was only ten. I remember the sweet smell of Cottonwood trees along the river and the coolness of the night air and the slippery rocks under my feet as we fished long after sundown, long after my Grandmother had proclaimed my bedtime. I remember coming back filled with the smell and feel of the fish and the river, comfortable with my Uncle's companionable silence and listening, only abstractly, to my Grandmother's scolding.

With only two months left now before my family reunion, I am still practicing re-membering. And it does take practice. I am grateful to The Talker (and still a little humiliated) for showing me how easily I can become ensnared. There is a trickiness, after all, in Spider Woman's teaching. She is Creatress. Creation, however, is not simply an action. It is a cycle of change. As Creatress, She begins *and* ends. She weaves *and* mends. She leaves us free to make our own choices and to receive the lessons of our actions. She teaches us that it is the process of creation to try over and over again.

 ## PRACTICE:
Re-membering

1. Listen for The Talker. Make a special page in your journal for Words of The Talker. Leave the back of this page blank. When the page is full, turn it over and change the story. If this is not possible for you to do, write The Talker's words over and over until they begin to feel tiresome to you. Then burn the paper/s and release the negativity.

2. Role play The Talker in circle
First complete the process of #1. Write out two or three sentences typical of The Talker. Work in twos. Take the part of the other person's Talker while they listen. Avoid dialogue. The point is to hear The Talker as outside of yourself. Follow by freewriting or passing the talking stick.

3. Choosing to Re-member: Spider gives the gift of memory (connection to the past) and of re-membering (recreating your interpretation of the past). Both are selective and, at least to some extent, subject to choice. For example, I *choose* to process and let go of negative experience rather than carry its weight. At the same time, I keep the wisdom of that experience. I *choose* to re-member that experience from the vantage point of the wisdom rather than the pain.

Go back to the pattern found in "Spider Woman Mandalas," #1, Web of Connection.

Choose one "world" to work with—e.g. work, family of origin, friends/lovers, primary family. Using the circle pattern and self as center, place the important people around you in the circle, close or far indicative of relationship. Draw and color in the lines of connection you feel with each. Draw and color in lines of connection between the people as well. Let these lines reflect the quality and tone of the relationships (as you feel them).

Choose one of the relationships (or relationship complexes) that pulls you emotionally. Freewrite your feelings about the relationship. Leave the freewriting for at least a day before re-reading it.

Read the freewrite and underline where you hear The Talker. Follow instructions in number 1 (above) for processing the negativity.

On a new sheet of paper, write what you choose to re-member, including the lessons learned, the wisdom.

 MAKING RITE:

"Dance of the Butterfly Maidens": Today I walked in the garden, watching the butterflies and thinking of the "Butterfly Maidens" from the Creation Song in the Book of the Hopi. It was hard *not* to think of the song, so joyous was the butterfly dance in the moment of sparkling sunshine between rain showers. The dance seemed to go like this:

Butterfly representing cycle of birth-death-rebirth. Mycenae, sixteenth century BCE

I am one
flying in the sunshine
in the flowers, in the sparkling dew
I am one
swooping and soaring
hovering and touching
whatever I choose to do.

I meet you
We fly, two by two
We fly together
swooping and soaring
hovering and touching
together we move as two.

Then we let go and I am one
flying in the sunshine
lighting on the flower
swooping and soaring
whatever my impulse to do

until I meet you and we fly
in joy feeling our rhythms
dancing together we soar.

One and together, one and together, the butterflies danced, always connected to self and to source.

In Circle:

You need: space to dance, a trunk of fanciful scarves and clothes, light, airy music (e.g. Gabrielle Roth's "lyrical" rhythm, harp or flute music...) and your child self. Give direction to dress fancifully as a butterfly. Suggest to the circle that they are in a garden of sunlight and flowers and to move as their butterfly self desires, soaring, swooping, lighting, hovering—feeling the joy of being. When they meet another, they join dances until the impulse comes to separate and dance as one. Continue until the circle lets go into the rhythm of one, together, one, together. Complete by journaling or passing the talking stick.

 IN YOUR MUSE:

In your particular art form, create a portrait of "The Butterly Maidens."

Add image cards to your Spider Woman Deck.

The Face of Spider Woman

In early spring, I asked you, Spider Mother, to show me your face. Now as summer solstice approaches, after months of writing and dwelling with you, I have begun to feel that looking into your face is like looking into the wheel of change itself, or entering one of the jewels of Indra's web, infinitely reflecting. So many faces you have, all connected, all reflecting the others. Goddess Triune are you, turning wheel. Slowly, I begin to understand the lesson you have taught me through the years—that the process of creating is about changing.

An artist friend asks me, "How is the book coming?" "I am still writing about Spider," I reply. "It would be a lot easier if I didn't have to grow as well as write." We both laugh, a laugh of mutual catharsis and understanding. Have I ever engaged in a creative process without finding myself looking more deeply into my own face? Recently, I was part of a Creativity Class. "In the next few hours, your assignment is to journey into the forest guided by your impulse until you feel like you have gone beyond your comfort zone in some way," the teacher told us, "until you feel like you are *on the edge*. Observe your thoughts and attitudes during the process," she added.

"How will I do *that?*" I wondered, "I know this forest so well." I noted the attitude and began walking the back hills, heading in a different direction than usual. I walked until the forest was unfamiliar, until I felt the possibility that something unexpected might happen. I didn't know what—but that was the point. I experienced a palpable feeling of *not having been here before*. With it came an alertness, an aliveness, and an undercurrent of fear. As I sat down to journal my experiences, I realized that I had been led into experiencing physically the terrain of creativity—a place where the new arises, often amidst a swirl of fear.

Teaching, mothering, and loving shaped who I was in my first fifty years. They were the expression of my creativity. In living them, I experienced depths of birthing and dying as well as expanses of growing. Then in my 52nd year, all the structures of that life crumbled beneath me and I gave up a comfortable lifestyle to begin a creative project that took me to the edge both in resources and credibility. In fact, more than one of my professional associates thought I had gone *over* the edge. They asked: "Isn't it rather late in your life to do something like this?" (living on the land, homesteading) I was supposed to retire to a cozy apartment rather than a 8x10 shed in the forest with no electricity, no running water, let alone hot water, and no toilet. And then to share this with other inhabitants of the forest—rats, mice, squirrels, ants, bees, termites...who unrelentingly claimed it as their own. All that was absurd enough, but that I, a fifty-five year old woman with no skills and no experience in construction (and no money to pay for help) should start building a retreat center in the forest—this was surely the scenario of failure.

My family just laughed, "She won't be able to build a place out there. She can't even hammer a nail!" I learned. Locals of this coastal area, seasoned by its hardships, just shook their heads, "She won't last." I lasted—through rodent wars, floods, cold and wet. And MUD. For once we had disturbed the forest floor by digging the footing for The Forest House, we had clay mud with the sucking capacity of a giant Bootsnatcher. Often I thought of the Charlie Chaplin classics of the Old West, landscapes of black and gray where downcast pioneers slog around in the rain, mud knee deep, coping with one catastrophe after another. Cold and discouragement are still very real in my body, but also a strength born of endurance. Sometimes I wonder, however, if the endurance came from passion for the goal or simply from having made the LEAP, having invested everything, emotional as well as financial.

During those years, my family and friends were also puzzled and a little worried, some even "scandalized," by my close friendship with a Lesbian, a Coyote Woman familiar with the art of leaps into the impossible. Together, we had fallen in love with the goddess—watching our lives change and swirl around us. We shared magic and dream time. Together we had asked in ritual to do the work of the goddess/earth. When the forest we called Wanderland appeared, we gave everything we had. We started doing tie dye to pay for a project that had no end in sight, but began by trading my comfortable house as the down payment for a forest. Clothes scruffy, hands stained purple with dye and roughened with work, I lived part time in an unfinished attic in the city that I shared with my Lesbian friend and part time in a one room shed in the midst of a forest—and worked, shovel by shovel, board by board to build something that might make a difference. "Has she lost her mind?" people asked, "living like that. Maybe it's drugs, or maybe she's become a *lesbian,* or a *hippie,* at 55?"

I have told the story of this experience in many different ways over the last eleven years, for there are so *many* ways to tell it. My first book was born in the attic and the shed. Now as I sit in the comfort of The Forest House with electricity and hot baths and a word processor, I know that, although the project is not yet complete, much of the hardship is a story of the past. Wanderland Rainforest has become a retreat place and a teaching forest. And what have I become? I have created something but it has equally created me. It is as if the goddess had chosen exactly the creative project needed to force me to grow beyond the fears that confine me: Fear of other's judgment and disapproval. Fear of looking unattractive—dirty, messy, poor. Fear of being alone. Fear of my life being out of control, of going irretrievably into debt—of failing.

And fail we did, again and again. For the creating was a process over time, an evolution—not simply a matter of going directly to the goal. In fact even the goal, itself, seemed to change as we understood more clearly what was being born. In this way, the project was similar to the work of Spider Woman who creates again and again, letting go of what does not work. Does she fail, or are the "worlds" she ends a pattern in the weaving? Our challenge was to figure out how to support ourselves and at the same time, keep the forest alive. For the forest was our reason for being there. For awhile we thought we might create a Permaculture farm, a philosophy based on cooperating with the patterns of the earth. Then we discovered that the forest—the wet, shade, rot, acid soil, slugs, rodents, deer, elk—ate most everything we planted. The dream of a blueberry farm disappeared; the dream of a mushroom farm disappeared; the dream of a lily farm disappeared, and so did many others. Until we finally realized that the forest had its *own* Permaculture. Still, each "failure" left its teaching and with that teaching a new door opened. This has happened so many times, with so many promising ideas, that by now I know a "failure" is not the end, but a necessary step into what is next. When people ask me about the huge blimp shaped piece of equipment, laced with berry vines at the end of our drive, I don't see the failure, instead I reply, "It's a leftover from when we thought we were becoming a mushroom farm, an autoclave on its way to a new home."

From the beginning, we had wanted somehow to show that the forest was valuable for the gifts it offered. We dreamed that if we could do this, the surrounding acres on our hillside would not be clear-cut. Maybe if we showed money could be made growing mushrooms instead of clear cutting. Maybe if we showed that natural forest products were a good business, as well as board feet. Maybe if we became an environmental learning center...Looking back, I know there was a great deal of naiveté in our attitude. We underestimated the size and the power of the Goliath devouring the forests of the Coast Range. Still this is what propelled us, and what continues to do so. When you love a place, property lines do not ease your pain at its destruction. I lived on the edge. I was in love with a forest that might be sacrificed at any moment. In addition, I discovered that the creek bordering Wanderland, wild and beautiful as it is, might be dammed in the near future to provide water for the city of Nehalem. It was this trick of fate, this falling in love with paradise on the brink of destruction, that forced me to walk into one of my deepest fears—facing the power of Patriarchal Authority.

It is hard to know where this fear began: perhaps in my childhood, where I was surrounded by male elders—grandfathers, uncles, Father—whose opinions and attitudes superseded those of the women in the family; perhaps from an innate shyness and sensitivity that feared the blast of male anger that always left me powerless and in tears. Or maybe it was the imprint of the culture itself, centuries of male power that shaped both attitude and function of every institution I entered from churches to government to academia. Or maybe it was even broader than that, rooted in the years of my birth when depression and war overpowered my parents' lives, and they lived in fear and helplessness, knowing they could not control their fate or the fate of their children. Even though many would not even suspect its existence, the root of this fear goes deeply in me. It goes even farther back than this lifetime, welling up in memory of women who were beaten, hung, burned—the memory so vivid it is me crying out in pain: "The earth is alive! The earth is sacred!" as the cold voice of The Judge proclaims, "Enough."

Several years ago, I spent close to sixty hours working on a grant proposal for funding environmental classes at Wanderland Rainforest. It was an interdisciplinary approach bringing in a variety of teachers who viewed nature from many angles: science, art, personal and spiritual relationship. The response I received from the Watershed Council was "this is not scientific enough," "this is not a watershed proposal." "Try rewriting it. Take out emotional and spiritual phrasing like 'story telling,' 'circles,' 'fire-circle,' 'maskmaking'." I could not. The fish biologist who had agreed to work on the project quit. The proposal dropped by the wayside. For awhile I was angry and defeated. Then I realized that the experience clarified for me what our project *was* about: nature is *not* separate from spirit. We continued to do what it was we believed in doing. In the practice of that, I grow stronger. In the practice of that, I also learn ways of speaking that do not polarize others with their own fears.

Perhaps the hardest part for me is speaking out in strength and clarity—for the forest, for the creek, for the ocean, for the animals—in forums and in conversations where the dominant view is that *human right* precedes all else.

The work of John Seed and Joanna Macy have helped me immeasurably in overcoming my personal fear of this. One of their books is called "Speaking Like a Mountain" And this is exactly the point. The animals, the forests, the creeks cannot speak for themselves in human councils that decide their fate. Who else but you will speak? If you love them, speak for them as you would for your loved ones. Why do they have the right to live?

The project is not finished yet, and neither am I. This is clear to me. Somewhere I once read that if a creative project takes longer than two years, it is about the journey not the goal. This project is as large as my lifetime. But that is only as far as I can see. Spider Woman—She knows how many worlds are in the weaving. She knows the infinity of the creative source as she turns the wheel, as she weaves from the loom at the center of the tree of life.

 PRACTICE:
The Creative Edge

1. Free-form doodling: Create a portrait of yourself in relationship to a creative project you are thinking about (or have begun). Symbolize strengths and fears with color, size, and shape.

2. Track your emotions and attitudes toward your creative project, journaling each

night over a period of time. Notice how you describe it to others, be particularly aware of apology, negativity, self-put-down. What are the fears the project brings up? Freewrite on each, exploring in more depth. Or do a landscape of each fear.

3. Take a major fear brought up by your creative project and work with it as an initiation. Sketch a gateway that symbolizes the initiation meeting this fear asks of you. Symbolically represent yourself before passing through this gateway. Then sketch yourself having passed through the gateway to the other side. What changes has passing through the fear brought about?

Add images to your Spider Woman Deck.

WILD CARDS
Playing with the SPIDER WOMAN DECK

You have now completed the Spider Woman Deck. Images in this deck reflect the many faces of the Creatress within you and your ability to manifest your visions. Spider Woman teaches you about connections—beginning, ending, and re-membering. Shuffle the deck and pull four cards, a fifth if you choose. Arrange the cards in any way you desire...in a sequence, a circle, a collage...Feel free to discard and draw again. Freewrite the story of the cards. Follow your Muse in going deeper.

In Circle

1. If you are working with a circle, shuffle everyone's images together and use them like a deck of cards, passing them around for everyone to choose from until they are gone. Follow the same process of laying them out in sequence and telling or sketching their story. You can also invent rules. A "discard" pile might be interesting where you can get rid of one but must take another. Play around.

2. In a circle, play around with the images through aspecting and improvisational drama. Each choose an image. Get into the energy—dress like it, move like it, sound like it. A group of eight or so doing this with different aspects at once is wildly energizing! Afterwards, pass the talking stick or write in your journal. What did the experience feel like in your body?

This mandala of Spider the Creatress, carved on shell, was found, in a burial mound in Oklahoma. It is a "gorget," a shield, that was worn by Native women around 13 C.E. It reminds us that we, too, are the weavers, the makers of our reality.

EPILOGUE

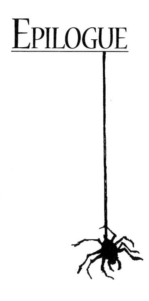

A Family Reunion

In mid-August my family gathered for the first time since my father's death seven years ago. There were about forty of us—my brothers, their children, and their childrens' children; my own children and grandchildren, and several of my cousins. We are a remarkably diverse group. Not only do we live in different parts of the country, but we also inhabit different landscapes of mind and spirit. This not only makes it difficult for us to understand each other, but sometimes we even forget that we love each other—until we see the other and that sudden recognition bursts from our hearts. But then what?

I had worried for several months about this gathering for it was to be held at Wanderland. Even though I have lived here for over ten years, most of my relatives, including two of my brothers, had never been here. Wanderland is beautiful. It is also an environmental and spiritual statement. For months, vague worries knotted my stomach. Would I be able to avoid political, environmental, and religious disagreements? Should I dismantle the house of alters and masks–images of the goddess? What if it rained—how would 40 people (including 15 small children) fit in The Forest House? And then, there was my Malamute, Luna, who didn't like children at all—and who, in her old age, tended to be unpredictable, even with adults, in her space. By the morning of the reunion, I had thought of just about everything that could go wrong—from every possible angle. And yet I entirely missed what actually happened.

The morning dawned beautiful and clear, a perfect August day in the forest. But the focus of my worry had shifted. For three days Luna had grown increasingly weak and uncomfortable. She no longer made the trip up the stairs of the house for her meals, nor did she lumber into the car for the trips to town that had been the highlight of her day. Instead, she had dug an imprint in the earth under the deck, a shallow bed where she lay. I had started her on a high powered antibiotic the day before, hoping, as the Vet said, it would clear up the urinary tract infection that seemed to grow increasingly worse. At the moment, all that gave her comfort was me stroking her and talking to her.

By noon, my younger brother arrived with a carload of little grandchildren and, then it seemed the whole place began to blossom with the many members of my family I had not seen for years. "Don't approach the dog under the deck," I warned people, "She is sick and very grumpy." And so she was as if encased by invisible walls, as children ran all around her, in and out of the forest, up and down the steps. I remember the day through a blur of emotion, my heart moved by memories—my brothers, so familiar, yet strangers as well, nieces and nephews whom I remembered as little children, grown into parents of little children I had never met before, and in between the hugs and the tours of the forest, always there was Luna, lying under the deck, waiting for my touch and the reassuring words I, myself, did not believe. My heart began to split open. I was not capable of anything besides concern—and love.

Through the haze, I began to hear the voices of my family: "The forest is so lovely..." "Thank you for inviting us into your sacred space." We shared pictures and memories and old movies of our grandparents. By the next day, the gathering had its own momentum, and, it was understood, that I was keeping company under the deck with my old friend, Luna. "I know how you feel," one by one they told me. "I had a dog I loved—and lost." And then they would share the story. By this time, I no longer even tried to control my tears. Luna was dying. And she had exposed me as starkly human in the midst of my family. I do not think that any one of us changed our political, environmental, or religious views during those two days. I do know I was totally incapable of such discussions. It may even be another seven years before we all gather again, but I do not recall one disagreement or unpleasant remark. What I remember is the support and love; what I remember is how much my family always loved dogs.

Three days later, I made the decision to help Luna die. With her death, a whole chapter of my life unreeled before me—for we had walked together for almost 13 years. In her dying, she taught me that when your heart splits open from grief at losing one you love—it does not matter who or what—you walk between the worlds. This is the story of that passing.

Wild Spirit Passing

It was a warm August night, a full moon night, when Luna rose for the last time and walked painfully across the garden. She found a mossy spot about twenty feet from my tent—and I knew she had chosen a place to die. I would have welcomed her in my tent, or even my bed on this, our last night together, but in her usual Malamutish way, she chose her own space.

I first met Luna when she was six weeks old, an irresistible blue-eyed pup. "She's an Alpha female," I was warned as I chose her from a pile of thirteen sleeping puppies, "first born of the litter." It was her smile that caught me; then she opened her eyes and there was no going back. I hadn't a clue what she would teach me—of power and wildness and claiming your own space. She was my constant companion through a time of great change in my life. When other relationships fell away, she was always there. She was one year old when we walked for the first time into the forest I call Wanderland. She knew it immediately as "home"—jumping onto a stump, she took a long look around her and flashed me a Malamute grin as if to say, "Well, here we are, at last!" Over many years, as The Forest House slowly took shape, we lived pretty much the same lifestyle—sharing food cooked over the campfire, wrestling for the best spot in the tent, both wearing coats smudged with dirt and rain.

Even after the house was finished, I would abandon it during the warm summer months, so deeply at home I felt sleeping on the earth, bathed in the sounds of the creek and early morning birdsongs. She, on the other hand, seemed to think it a bit peculiar to abandon a lofty deck, a comfortable bed, and a refrigerator filled with food to sleep in a little dome tent. I cannot say that she was never judgmental. Still, night after night, she slept nearby, her steady breathing, a life pulse, always there. I could not imagine her gone. Yet, on this night, in the moment that she chose a place to die, I felt the fear that had clenched my heart all week, the fear that she was dying, release. In the absence of hope, the Death Goddess came. It was as if both our faces turned toward Her. "Give me the strength and courage to help her through," I prayed.

Under the full moon, I sang to you
stroking your face,
your beautiful Malamute face.
And you, who were sometimes snarly
were soft as the moonlight
and glowed back to me your love.

I sang the song that called you
from your place beneath the deck
to join our Lammas circle the week before.
I did not want to know then
why you came.

"Return to who you are,
Return to what you are,
Return again,
Return again,
Return to the land of your birth."

Under my hands, you fell asleep.
And I went to my tent
hands full of the touch of you.
I must remember this, I thought,
drifting in the moonlit night
listening...

I do not know if I slept. I only know I was startled by the sound of an animal crying. At first, I did not recognize her voice for it was a tremula song, a song to cougar and coyote that the time had come. Cougar and coyote both inhabit this forest, but I knew it would be me who must bring her death and release her from the pain. Still there were many hours yet before dawn and more still before I could make the call to the Vet for help. Wrapped in a blanket, again I sat beside her in the moonlight, stroking her face, telling her how beautiful she was, remembering with her the things she loved most in this life. "I'll meet you there," I told her. "It will just be a blink of the eye." She listened, blue eyes clear, knowing.

What I had thought would be an endless night was instead a sifting of time. Moon and stars like sand through my fingers vanished into morning and I heard the sound of Richard's truck coming up the driveway. "Give me the courage and strength to do this," I prayed. Between the two of us, I had thought we could carry her the hundred feet across the garden to my car. But her 115 lbs. became even heavier with her resistance to being moved. We rolled her into a sleeping bag and dragged her, snarling and crying in pain. In her pain and fear she bit at everything along the way and caught my hand. I grabbed some plantain from along the path to stop the bleeding. Once in the car, she calmed, for this was her nest and I sat with her a few moments before we began the forty mile trip to our 11 o'clock appointment with death.

When I made the call to the Vet I had asked that the shot be given to her in the car for it was her home. When I walked into the office, however, I was asked to move the car closer to the "backyard window" so they could lower an apparatus to strap and muzzle her. "No," I replied, holding my bleeding hand behind me, "We are not doing that. I will hold her. You come in from the other side." Reluctantly, they agreed to try.

Luna had known where we were the moment we arrived. Nose straight in the air, the smell told her everything. I imagine that memories flooded through her—the broken leg at three months, the spaying, the staph infection, and all the other indignities that had been accompanied by that smell. She hated the vet. Still when I got into the back seat beside her, she simply snuggled into me. I held her only lightly. Looking back, I saw her back leg extended as if she were offering it. These moments seemed longer than the whole night had been. "You are so beautiful," I told her over and over. She did not even flinch when the needle went into her vein. She simply merged with me—as she did when I first held her as a puppy.

"She's gone," the vet said. Still, I held her, feeling her weight against me, and when, finally, I eased out from under her and let her head fall to rest on her paws, I could still feel the warmth vibrating in my center. And so it was long after, in the strangely quiet car, driving her body back home, her warmth still inside of me.

An hour later, I walked into the house with my hand still bleeding as the phone rang. I answered automatically, thinking it to be my concerned daughter. "I want to register for a workshop," the voice said. "Can I call you back," I asked. I've cut myself and I need to take care of it," I lied, unwilling to explain that my dog had bitten me badly as I took her to her death and that now she lay dead in my car. I hung up and wrapped a bandage around my hand. "I have to get her out of my car," I thought, at the same time not knowing how I would move a dog the size of a person a hundred feet down the forest trail to the grave my son had dug for her the week before.

When I opened the car door, she looked so life-like, for an irrational moment I thought her eyebrows were going to move and I was going to freak out. It was then I learned the value of "dead weight," for in my hands, I felt her heavy and knew her as dead. Slowly I maneuvered her body from the car and inch by inch down the forest trail, talking to her all the way about the turns and obstacles and bumps. Her head faced North in the grave as I snuggled the sleeping bag around her and stroked her face one last time. "You will have an Indian burial," I said, putting in her bones, the last of the weiners she loved, and her favorite toys.

I was not far into shoveling the dirt back into the grave, when I became aware of how badly my injured hand was hurting. "I need help," I thought. "Who can I call?" I walked back into the house and picked up the phone to find a message from my friend, Terry. "I heard you cut your hand," he said. "Do you need help?" I dialed his number and left him a return message: "I'm OK. I just need help filling in the grave." Not until

I was back outside did I realize how strange that must have sounded, but I was beyond trying to correct it. I went to my tent and lay there letting go of my body, exhausted, drifting into semi-consciousness. "Go to the Goddess Iris," I heard, but did not understand.

The sound of Terry's truck coming up the drive called me, reluctantly, out of the tent and back to the reality of filling a grave. In a short time, Terry, who always proves to be some kind of teacher-in-disguise, was showing me how to fill in a grave with grace and sureness, all the time talking of his beautifully crafted new shovel. When he was done, even the rawness of the fresh earth was smoothed. I collapsed into a chair near the garden, listening to his truck going back down the driveway.

"Now I am all alone," I thought. "I have never been at Wanderland without Luna." I expected silence and aloneness to flood through me. Instead, the garden was filled with golden light. Butterflies and hummingbirds dipped in and out of flowers. The flowers were glowing. A bird was singing. I glanced at The Forest House. It, too, glowed with golden light. "I am in the garden of Paradise," I thought, rising to walk across the garden. Close to the deck where Luna loved to sleep, I was startled by a black snake, at least two and a half feet long, with bright orange triangles along its sides. It crossed the flower bed; then turned and came back again, while I stood unable to move.

"That I am alone is obviously delusion," I said aloud. And suddenly I had the answer to a question I have been continually asked since moving to the forest: "Do you live out here all by yourself?" "Do you live here *alone?*" One of the gifts on this day of Luna's passing was the answer: *"No. I live here along with everything else."*

Before I slept in the tent that evening, I walked the path where we had dragged Luna to the car, smudging it with sage and chanting "May the fear and pain be gone; may the fear and pain be banished. Heal this way and take her spirit free." That night I slept deeply, only occasionally startled by animal cries, and then knowing they were not hers. In the night, I dreamt that Luna was passing down a tunnel, her reel leash, which I held, extended far beyond its capacity. She was beyond my holding her. Then I was sitting at a table talking to a friend. "I think Luna is doing the escalator-tunnel without me," I said.

The next day, I finally remembered to look up the Goddess Iris. "Greek Goddess of the rainbow," I read, "personifying like the Hindu Maya, the many-colored veils of the world's appearances behind which the spirit of the Goddess worked unseen. *In many mythologies she personified the bridge between earth and heaven, the Rainbow Bridge.* Like the part of the eye named after her, she was a form of the Great Shakti who was both the organ of sight and the visible world that it saw." [1] I felt so blessed, so cared for, in the middle of my grief and not knowing. I did not know how to go to Her. She came to me—in the Beauty of the garden, in the golden glow that surrounded and made me part-of, not alone.

In the days that followed, I made a garden on the earth under which she lay, things that reminded me of her, shells from her favorite beaches, gravel from under the deck, her watering bowl half covered so that its aluminum shone like a moon. I made a sign of cedar for a tree near-by that said simply: "Wild Spirit Passing." The process was necessary for me and it seemed as if she sat nearby, smiling. Several weeks later, a friend unexpectedly brought a stone from Neahkahnie Mountain, so heavy it took the two of us to carry it from her car. Engraved on its flat surface were the three phases of the moon and under them "LUNA, GUARDIAN OF WANDERLAND."

Luna and Gwendolyn, 1993

AFTERWORD

Twelve Ways to Surf Emotion

1. Breathe. The natural inflow, outflow of breath cleanses the body and helps us to let go of tension and emotion. Joanna Macy teaches a simple breath she calls "breathing through" that not only helps release emotion as it comes up from memory of past experience, but also helps you to stay sensitive and responsive to present experience without storing the pain in your body. It goes like this:

Relax. Center on your breathing. Visualize your breath as a stream flowing up through your nose, down through your windpipe and lungs. Take it down through your lungs and, picturing an opening in the bottom of your heart, out through that hole to connect with the larger web of life around you. Let the breath-stream, as it passes through you, appear as one loop in the vast web, connecting you with it...keep breathing.

Breathe in the pain (or whatever you are feeling) like a dark stream, up through your nose, down through your trachea, lungs, and heart and out again into the world net... You are asked to do nothing for now, but let it pass through and out again; don't hang on to the pain. Surrender it to the healing resources of life's vast web." *Despair and Empowerment in the Nuclear Age,* Joanna Macy

2. Free write in your journal. Don't censor. Let whatever comes out, come out. Remember that it may not be in words.

3. Write a dialogue with your emotion. This process not only distances you from the emotion, it often gives you insight into it. To do this, you simply name the emotion; speak to it as if it is separate from you; then let it answer. Follow first impulse on this. Don't try to figure it out. Let the dialogue continue as long as there is momentum behind it.

4. If the emotion arises from an interaction with someone in your past, write a letter in your journal or a dialogue with them.

5. Use sound. Breathe, find the place in your body where you feel the emotion. Inhale, allow a sound to move through this place on the exhale. Inhale and again sound and exhale through the place in your body where you feel the emotion.

6. Use dance or movement to express the emotion.

7. Make a mask that represents the emotion you are feeling. Dance or act out the feeling with the mask.

8. If you are releasing anger, try a plastic bat and a big pillow, then let fly.

9. If you are feeling grief or sorrow, try curling up with a large soft pillow, holding it close to your center.

10. Do a water cleansing: You will need a safe space where you can make whatever sounds you wish. Place a bowl of water in front of you (you may wish to use sea salt or crystals in the water). Breathe and ground. Allow yourself time to come into your body and feel your emotions. Breathe and release the emotion with sound, seeing it in your mind's eye, propelled into the cleansing water. As it hits the water, see it transform into light. Continue the process until you feel it is completed. Give the water back to the earth.

If you do not wish to go into the emotion, respect that. Shift focus.

11. Let the earth heal you. Go for a walk in the forest, or by the ocean. Spend time in the garden, or listen to the birds singing in your back yard.

12. Go biking, or walking, or running, or swimming, or take a luxurious bath. Nurture yourself.

Always honor your own timing, your own rhythms, that you grow in your own way. At the same time, honor emotions for they are teachers—teachers of what it is to be alive and sensitive in body; teachers of what it is to respond to experience. Through emotion, we learn what we can and cannot do. We learn what situations are nurturing to us and what ones are not. We learn what we wish to choose and what we wish to change.

Inner Dance by Diana Mariechild is an excellent self help book for journeying into emotion with breath and active imagination. In addition Joanna Macy's *Despair and Empowerment in The Nuclear Age* is invaluable in teaching how to reclaim both our sensitivity and our personal power. For journaling exercises that allow you to explore emotion see Tristine Rainer's *New Diary.*

Surfing

If I could remember
  to be a surfer
  riding the tides of emotion
  feeling as I go

If I could remember
  to be a surfer
  feel, breathe,
  and let go

I could be
  surfing feeling
  as I grow
  feeling as I grow.

> *gwendolyn*

Notes

INTRODUCTION

1. RUDI HURZLMEIER AUS DER REHE: "KOMISHE VOGEL" KRAHE 4708, " Inkognito. Last known address: Erkelenzdamm 11-13, 10999, Berlin. A search was made for this artist in three different languages.

STORY ONE

1. The Coyote story included here is a retelling of "Coyote and the Cedar Tree" as it appears in *Coyote Was Going There* by Jarold Ramsey, 1976, p. 133ff.
2. Jose and Miriam Arguelles, *Mandala*, 1985, p. 60.
3. Carl Jung, *Mandala Symbolism*, 1973, p.5.
4. Robert Lawler, *Voices of the First Day*, 1991. p. 387.
5. Lawlor, p. 87.
6. Sandra Ingerman, *Soul Retrieval*, 1995, p. 187.
7. Clarissa Pinkola Estes, *Women Who Run with the Wolves*, 1992.
8. Ingerman, p. 187.

STORY TWO

1. Barbara Walker, *The Woman's Encyclopedia of Myth and Secret*, 1983, p. 701.
2. Meinrad Craighead, *The Mother's Songs*, 1986, p. 55.
3. "Ice and White Sea Otter Woman" is a retelling of the story as found in Clara Pearson, *Nehalem Tillamook Tales*, edited by Elizabeth and Melville Jacobs, 1990.
4. John Neihardt, *Black Elk Speaks*, 1932, p. 4-5.
5. Hallie Inglehart Austen, *The Heart of the Goddess*, 1990, p.56.
6. Mara Freeman, "Enchanted Beasts and Faerie Women," *Parabola*, Fall 1999, p. 29.
7. Ruth Underhill, *Singing for Power*, 1938, p. 53-54.
8. Underhill, p. 45.
9. Michael Phillips, *Legend of the Celtic Stone*, 1999, p. 231-232.
10. Phillips, p. 232.
11. Gwendolyn Endicott, *The Spinning Wheel*, 1994, p.67.
12. John Sauter and Bruce Johnson, *The Tillamook Indians*, 1972, p. 120.
13. Vinson Brown, *Pacific Coast Sea Mammals*, 1959, p. 84.
14. Estes, p. 262.
15. Carolyn McVickar Edwards, *Storyteller's Goddess*, 1991, p. 99.
16. Dennis Tedlock and Barbara Tedlock, *Teachings from the American Earth*, 1975, p. 16.
17. Tedlock, p. 16.
18. Walker, p. 200.
19. Walker, p. 199.
20. Lawlor, 113-114.

STORY THREE

1. William Brandon, *The Magic World*, 1971, p. 69.
2. Mary Beck, *Heroes and Heroines in Tlingit -Haida Legend,*
3. Donna Wilshire, *Virgin, Mother, Crone*, 1994, p. 196.
4. Beck, p. 43.
5. Wilshire, p. 259.
6. Hallie Inglehart Austen, *Heart of the Goddess,* p. 68.
7. Ed Ayres, "God's Last Offer," *Resurgence*, January/February 2000, p. 64.
8. Thomas Moore, "The Presence of Spirits," *Resurgence,* January/February 2000, p. 34.

STORY FOUR

1. "Spider Woman and the Making of the Worlds," is a retelling of the Creation Story as found in Frank Waters, *The Book of the Hopi,* 1970. p. 1-27.
2. Marie-Louise von Franz, *Time*, 1978, p. 32.
3. Joseph Bruchak, *The Soul of Nature,* 1994, p.100.
4. Bruchak
5. Starhawk, *The Fifth Sacred Thing,* 1993, p. 225.
6. Starhawk, p. 226.
7. Waters, p. 22.
8. Estes, p. 194.
9. James G. Cowan, *The Aborigine Tradition,* 1992, p. 90.
10. Frank Waters, *Masked Gods,* 1970, 258ff.
11. Cowan, p. 90.

The Artists

Barbara Matson
P.O. Box 1285
Borrego Springs, California 92004

Barbara Temple-Ayres
jta@nehalemtel.net

Carolyn Greenwood
CarolynG@hevanet.com

Clayton Rippey
Cezanne Gallery International
P.O. Box 2354,
Bakersfield, California 93303
661/325-1336
claymar22@yahoo.com

Craig Spegel
503/368-5653

Gary Braasch
braasch@nehalemtel.net

Gwendolyn Endicott
gwendolyn@nehalemtel.net

Joe Balden
baldjg@nehalemtel.net

Lane de Moll
38755 Reed Road
Nehalem, Oregon 97131
lane@nehalemtel.net

Liza Jones
P. O. Box 327
Manzanita, Oregon 97130
maxduck@nehalemtel.net

Lola Sorensen
lola@nehalemtel.net

Lorraine Ortiz
The Art Ranch
39450 North Fork Road
Nehalem, Oregon 97131
lortiz@nehalemtel.net

Marilyn Burkhardt
P.O. Box D
Hebo, Oregon 97122
marilyn@athomeonearth.com
www.athomeonearth.com

Sam Harmon
11030 Ocean Way
Nehalem, Oregon 97131
503/368-4844
skygarden@nehalemtel.net

Order Page

These books may be ordered directly from ATTIC PRESS .

THE SPINNING WHEEL, The Art of Mythmaking
by Gwendolyn Endicott

_____ copies @ $14 (includes shipping) $_____

CRONE TREKKING IN COYOTE LAND, A Storymaking Book
by Gwendolyn Endicott

_____ copies @ $16 (includes shipping) $_____

Shipping (postage paid when ordering direct) $_____ N/C _____

TOTAL ENCLOSED $_____

SHIP TO:

NAME _____

ADDRESS _____

CITY/STATE/ZIP _____

Mail order form and check or money order to:
ATTIC PRESS c/o Wanderland
42130 Anderson Rd., Nehalem, Oregon 97131

Contact us at: 503/368-6389
or on the web: www.wanderlandrainforest.org